SMALL SPACES

KATHERINE ARDEN

putnam

G. P. PUTNAM'S SONS

G. P. PUTNAM'S SONS
an imprint of Penguin Random House LLC
375 Hudson Street
New York, NY 10014

G. P. Putnam's Sons is a registered trademark of Penguin Random House LLC.

Library of Congress Cataloging-in-Publication Data
Names: Arden, Katherine, author.
Title: Small spaces / Katherine Arden.
Description: New York, NY : G. P. Putnam's Sons Books for Young Readers, [2018]
Summary: "After eleven-year-old Ollie's school bus mysteriously breaks down on a field trip,
she has to take a trip through scary woods, and must use all of her wits to survive.
She must stick to small spaces"—Provided by publisher.
Identifiers: LCCN 2018010780 | ISBN 9780525515029 (hardback) | ISBN 9780525515036 (ebook)
Subjects: | CYAC: Supernatural—Fiction. | Survival—Fiction. | Forests and forestry—Fiction. |
Friendship—Fiction. | Books and reading—Fiction. | BISAC: JUVENILE FICTION / Action & Adventure /
Survival Stories. | JUVENILE FICTION / Mysteries & Detective Stories.
Classification: LCC PZ7.1.A737 Sm 2018 | DDC [Fic]—dc23
LC record available at https://lccn.loc.gov/2018010780

Printed in the United States of America.
ISBN 9780525515029
1 3 5 7 9 10 8 6 4 2

Design by Jaclyn Reyes.
Text set in Dante MT Pro.

1

OCTOBER IN EAST EVANSBURG, and the last warm sun of the year slanted red through the sugar maples. Olivia Adler sat nearest the big window in Mr. Easton's math class, trying, catlike, to fit her entire body into a patch of light. She wished she were on the other side of the glass. You don't waste October sunshine. Soon the old autumn sun would bed down in cloud blankets, and there would be weeks of gray rain before it finally decided to snow. But Mr. Easton was teaching fractions and had no sympathy for Olivia's fidgets.

"Now," he said from the front of the room. His chalk squeaked on the board. Mike Campbell flinched. Mike Campbell got the shivers from squeaking blackboards and, for some reason, from people licking paper napkins. The sixth grade licked napkins around him as much as possible.

"Can anyone tell me how to convert three-sixteenths to a decimal?" asked Mr. Easton. He scanned the room for a victim. "Coco?"

"Um," said Coco Zintner, hastily shutting a sparkling pink notebook. "Ah," she added wisely, squinting at the board.

Point one eight seven five, thought Olivia idly, but she did not raise her hand to rescue Coco. She made a line of purple ink on her scratch paper, turned it into a flower, then a palm tree. Her attention wandered back to the window. *What if a vampire army came through the gates right now? Or no, it's sunny. Werewolves? Or what if the Brewsters' Halloween skeleton decided to unhook himself from the third-floor window and lurch out the door?*

Ollie liked this idea. She had a mental image of Officer Perkins, who got cats out of trees and filed police reports about pies stolen off windowsills, approaching a wandering skeleton. *I'm sorry, Mr. Bones, you're going to have to put your skin on—*

A large foot landed by her desk. Ollie jumped. Coco had either conquered or been conquered by three-sixteenths, and now Mr. Easton was passing out math quizzes. The whole class groaned.

"Were you paying attention, Ollie?" asked Mr. Easton, putting her paper on her desk.

"Yep," said Ollie, and added, a little at random, "point

2

one eight seven five." Mr. Bones had failed to appear. Lazy skeleton. He could have gotten them out of their math quiz.

Mr. Easton looked unconvinced but moved on.

Ollie eyed her quiz. *Please convert 9/8 to a decimal. Right.* Ollie didn't use a calculator or scratch paper. The idea of using either had always puzzled her, as though someone had suggested she needed a spyglass to read a book. She scribbled answers as fast as her pencil could write, put her quiz on Mr. Easton's desk, and waited, half out of her seat, for the bell to ring.

Before the ringing had died away, Ollie seized her bag, inserted a crumpled heap of would-be homework, stowed a novel, and bolted for the door.

She had almost made it out when a voice behind her said, "Ollie."

Ollie stopped; Lily Mayhew and Jenna Gehrmann nearly tripped over her. Then the whole class was going around her like she was a rock in a river. Ollie trudged back to Mr. Easton's desk.

Why me, she wondered irritably. Phil Greenblatt had spent the last hour picking his nose and sticking boogers onto the seat in front of him. Lily had hacked her big sister's phone and screenshotted some texts Annabelle sent her boyfriend. The sixth grade had been giggling over them all day. And Mr. Easton wanted to talk to *her*?

Ollie stopped in front of the teacher's desk. "Yes? I turned in my quiz and everything so—"

Mr. Easton had a wide mouth and a large nose that drooped over his upper lip. A neatly trimmed mustache took up the tiny bit of space remaining. Usually he looked like a friendly walrus. Now he looked impatient. "Your quiz is letter-perfect, as you know, Ollie," he said. "No complaints on that score."

Ollie knew that. She waited.

"You should be doing eighth-grade math," Mr. Easton said. "At least."

"No," said Ollie.

Mr. Easton looked sympathetic now, as though he knew why she didn't want to do eighth-grade math. He probably did. Ollie had him for homeroom and life sciences, as well as math.

Ollie did not mind impatient teachers, but she did not like sympathy face. She crossed her arms.

Mr. Easton hastily changed the subject. "Actually, I wanted to talk to you about chess club. We're missing you this fall. The other kids, you know, really appreciated that you took the time to work with them on their opening gambits last year, and there's the interscholastic tournament coming up soon so—"

He went on about chess club. Ollie bit her tongue. She wanted to go outside, she wanted to ride her bike, and she didn't want to rejoin chess club.

When Mr. Easton finally came to a stop, she said, not quite meeting his eyes, "I'll send the club some links about opening gambits. Super helpful. They'll work fine. Um, tell everyone I'm sorry."

He sighed. "Well, it's your decision. But if you were to change your mind, we'd love—"

"Yeah," said Ollie. "I'll think about it." Hastily she added, "Gotta run. Have a good day. Bye." She was out the door before Mr. Easton could object, but she could feel him watching her go.

Past the green lockers, thirty-six on each side, down the hall that always smelled like bleach and old sandwiches. Out the double doors and onto the front lawn. All around was bright sun and cool air shaking golden trees: fall in East Evansburg. Ollie took a glad breath. She was going to ride her bike down along the creek as far and as fast as she could go. Maybe she'd jump in the water. The creek wasn't *that* cold. She would go home at dusk—sunset at 5:58. She had lots of time. Her dad would be mad that she got home late, but he was always worrying about something. Ollie could take care of herself.

Her bike was a Schwinn, plum-colored. She had locked it neatly to the space nearest the gate. No one in Evansburg would steal your bike—*probably*—but Ollie loved hers and sometimes people would prank you by stealing your wheels and hiding them.

She had both hands on her bike lock, tongue sticking out as she wrestled with the combination, when a shriek split the air. "It's *mine!*" a voice yelled. "Give it back! No—you can't touch that. NO!"

Ollie turned.

Most of the sixth grade was milling on the front lawn, watching Coco Zintner hop around like a flea—it was she who'd screamed. Coco would not have been out of place in a troop of flower fairies. Her eyes were large, slanting, and ice-blue. Her strawberry-blond hair was so strawberry that in the sunshine it looked pink. You could imagine Coco crawling out of a daffodil each morning and sipping nectar for breakfast. Ollie was a little jealous. She herself had a headful of messy brown curls and no one would ever mistake her for a flower fairy. *But at least,* Ollie reminded herself, *if Phil Greenblatt steals something from me, I'm big enough to sock him.*

Phil Greenblatt had stolen Coco's sparkly notebook. The one Coco had closed when Mr. Easton called on her. Phil was ignoring Coco's attempts to get it back—he was a foot taller than her. Coco was *tiny*. He held the notebook easily over Coco's head, flipped to the page he wanted, and snickered. Coco shrieked with frustration.

"Hey, Brian," called Phil. "Take a look at this."

Coco burst into tears.

Brian Battersby was the star of the middle school

6

hockey team even though he was only twelve himself. He was way shorter than Phil, but looked like he fit together better, instead of sprouting limbs like a praying mantis. He was lounging against the brick wall of the school building, watching Phil and Coco with interest.

Ollie started to get mad. No one *liked* Coco much—she had just moved from the city and her squeaky enthusiasm annoyed everyone. But really, make her cry in school?

Brian looked at the notebook Phil held out to him. He shrugged. Ollie thought he looked more embarrassed than anything.

Coco started crying harder.

Brian definitely looked uncomfortable. "Come on, Phil, it might not be me."

Mike Campbell said, elbowing Brian, "No, it's totally you." He eyed the notebook page again. "I guess it could be a dog that looks like you."

"Give it *back!*" yelled Coco through her tears. She snatched again. Phil was waving the notebook right over her head, laughing. The sixth grade was laughing too, and now Ollie could see what they were all looking at. It was a picture—a good picture, Coco could really draw—of Brian and Coco's faces nestled together with a heart around them.

Phil sat behind Coco in math class; he must have seen her drawing. Poor dumb Coco—why would you do that if you were sitting in front of nosy Philip Greenblatt?

"Come on, Brian," Mike was saying. "Don't you want to go out with Hot Cocoa here?"

Coco looked like she wanted to run away except that she really wanted her notebook back and Ollie had pretty much had enough of the whole situation, and so she bent down, got a moderate-sized rock, and let it fly.

Numbers and throwing things, those were the two talents of Olivia Adler. She'd quit the softball team last year too, but her aim was still on.

Her rock caught Brian squarely in the back of the head, dropped him *thump* onto the grass, and turned everyone's attention from Coco Zintner to her.

Ideally, Ollie would have hit Phil, but Phil was facing her and Ollie didn't want to put out an eye. Besides, she didn't have a lot of sympathy for Brian. He knew perfectly well that he was the best at hockey, and half the girls giggled about him, and he wasn't coming to Coco's rescue even though he'd more or less gotten her into this with his dumb friends and his dumb charming smile.

Ollie crossed her arms, thought in her mom's voice, *Well, in for a penny . . .*, hefted another rock, and said, "Oops. My hand slipped." The entire sixth grade was staring. The kids in front started backing away. A lot of them thought she had cracked since last year. "Um, seriously, guys," she said. "Doesn't *anyone* have anything better to do?"

Coco Zintner took advantage of Phil's distraction to

snatch her notebook back. She gave Ollie a long look, and darted away.

Ollie thought, *I'm going to have detention for a year,* and then Brian got up, spitting out dirt, and said, "That was a pretty good throw."

The noise began. Ms. Mouton, that day's lawn monitor, finally noticed the commotion. "Now," she said, hurrying over. "Now, now." Ms. Mouton was the librarian and she was not the best lawn monitor.

Ollie decided that she wasn't going to say sorry or anything. Let them call her dad, let them shake their heads, let them give her detention tomorrow. At least tomorrow the weather would change and she would not be stuck in school on a nice day, answering questions.

Ollie jumped onto her bike and raced out of the school yard, wheels spitting gravel, before anyone could tell her to stop.

2

SHE PEDALED HARD past the hay bales in the roundabout on Main Street, turned onto Daisy Lane, and raced past the clapboard houses, where jack-o'-lanterns grinned on every front porch. She aimed her bike to knock down a rotting gray rubber hand groping up out of the earth in the Steiners' yard, turned again at Johnson Hill, and climbed, panting, up the steep dirt road.

No one came after her. *Well, why would they,* Ollie thought. She was Off School Property.

Ollie let her bike coast down the other side of Johnson Hill. It was good to be alone in the warm sunshine. The river ran silver to her right, chattering over rocks. The fire-colored trees shook their leaves down around her. It wasn't *hot,* exactly—but warm for October. Just cool enough for jeans, but the sun was warm when you tilted your face to it.

The swimming hole was Ollie's favorite place. Not far

from her house, it had a secret spot on a rock half-hidden by a waterfall. That spot was *Ollie's*, especially on fall days. After mid-September, she was the only one who went there. People didn't go to swimming holes once the weather turned chilly.

Other than her homework, Ollie was carrying *Captain Blood* by Rafael Sabatini, a broken-spined paperback that she'd dug out of her dad's bookshelves. She mostly liked it. Peter Blood outsmarted everyone, which was a feature she liked in heroes, although she wished Peter were a girl, or the villain were a girl, or *someone* in the book besides his boat and his girlfriend (both named Arabella) were a girl. But at least the book had romance and high-seas adventures and other *absolutely not Evansburg* things. Ollie liked that. Reading it meant going to a new place where she wasn't Olivia Adler at all.

Ollie braked her bike. The ground by the road was carpeted with scarlet leaves; sugar maples start losing their leaves before other trees. Ollie kept a running list in her head of sugar maples in Evansburg that didn't belong to anyone. When the sap ran, she and her mom would—

Nope. No, they wouldn't. They could buy maple syrup.

The road that ran beside the swimming hole looked like any other stretch of road. A person just driving by wouldn't know the swimming hole was there. But, if you knew just where to look, you'd see a skinny dirt trail that went from the road to the water. Ollie walked her bike down the trail. The trees seemed to close in around her. Above was a white-railed bridge. Below, the creek paused in its trip down the mountain. It spread out, grew deep and quiet enough for swimming. There was a cliff for jumping and plenty of hiding places for one girl and her book. Ollie hurried. She was eager to go and read by the water and be alone.

The trees ended suddenly, and Ollie was standing on the bank of a cheerful brown swimming hole.

But, to her surprise, someone was already there.

A slender woman, wearing jeans and flannel, stood at the edge of the water.

The woman was sobbing.

Maybe Ollie's foot scuffed a rock, because the woman jumped and whirled around. Ollie gulped. The woman was pretty, with amber-honey hair. But she had circles under her eyes like purple thumbprints. Streaks of mascara had run down her face, like she'd been crying for a while.

"Hello," the woman said, trying to smile. "You surprised me." Her white-knuckled hands gripped a small, dark thing.

"I didn't mean to scare you," Ollie said cautiously.

Why are you crying? she wanted to ask. But it seemed impolite to ask that question of a grown-up, even if her face was streaked with the runoff from her tears.

The woman didn't reply; she darted a glance to the rocky path by the creek, then back to the water. Like she was looking out for something. Or someone.

Ollie felt a chill creep down her spine. She said, "Are you okay?"

"Of course." The woman tried to smile again. Fail. The wind rustled the leaves. Ollie glanced behind her. Nothing.

"I'm fine," said the woman. She turned the dark thing over in her hands. Then she said, in a rush, "I just have to get rid of this. Put it in the water. And then—" The woman broke off.

Then? What then? The woman held the thing out over the water. Ollie saw that it was a small black book, the size of her spread-out hand.

Her reaction was pure reflex. "You can't throw away a book!" Ollie let go of her bike and jumped forward. Part of her wondered, *Why would you come here to throw a book in the creek? You can donate a book.* There were donation boxes all over Evansburg.

"I have to!" snapped the woman, bringing Ollie up short. The woman went on, half to herself, "That's the bargain. Make the arrangements. Then give the book to the water." She gave Ollie a pleading look. "I don't have a choice, you see."

Ollie tried to drag the conversation out of crazy town.

"You can donate a book if you don't want it," she said firmly. "Or—or give it to someone. Don't just throw it in the creek."

"I *have* to," said the woman again.

"Have to drop a book in the creek?"

"Before tomorrow," said the woman. Almost to herself, she whispered, "Tomorrow's the day."

Ollie was nearly within arm's reach now. The woman smelled sour—frightened. Ollie, completely bewildered, decided to ignore the stranger elements of the conversation. Later, she would wish she hadn't. "If you don't want that book, I'll take it," said Ollie. "I like books."

The woman shook her head. "He said water. Upstream. Where Lethe Creek runs out of the mountain. I'm here. I'm *doing* it!" She shrieked the last sentence as though someone besides Ollie were listening. Ollie had to stop herself from looking behind her again.

"Why?" she asked. Little mouse feet crept up her spine.

"Who knows?" the woman whispered. "Just his game, maybe. He enjoys what he does, you know, and that is why he's always smiling—" She smiled too, a joyless pumpkin-head grin.

Ollie nearly yelped. But instead, her hand darted up and she snatched the book. It felt fragile under her fingers, gritty with dust. Surprised at her own daring, Ollie hurriedly backed up.

The woman's face turned red. "Give that back!" A glob of spit hit Ollie in the cheek.

"I don't think so," said Ollie. "You don't want it anyway." She was backing toward her bike, half expecting the woman to fling herself forward.

The woman was staring at Ollie as if really seeing her for the first time. "Why—?" A horrified understanding dawned on her face that Ollie didn't understand. "How old are you?"

Ollie was still backing toward her bike. "Eleven," she answered, by reflex. Almost there . . .

"Eleven?" the woman breathed. "Eleven. Of course, eleven." Ollie couldn't tell if the woman was giggling or crying. Maybe both. "It's his kind of joke—" She broke off, leaned forward to whisper. "Listen to me, Eleven. I'm going to tell you one thing, because I'm not a bad person. I just didn't have a choice. I'll give you some advice, and you give me the book." She had her hand out, fingers crooked like claws.

Ollie, poised on the edge of flight, said, "Tell me what?" The creek rushed and rippled, but the harsh sounds of the woman's breathing were louder than the water.

"Avoid large places at night," the woman said. "Keep to small."

"Small?" Ollie was torn between wanting to run and wanting to understand. "That's it?"

"Small!" shrieked the woman. *"Small spaces! Keep to small spaces or see what happens to you! Just see!"* She burst into wild laughter. The plastic witch sitting on the Brewsters' porch laughed like that. *"Now give me that book!"* Her laughter turned into a whistling sob.

Ollie heaved the Schwinn around and fled with it up the trail. The woman's footsteps scraped behind. "Come back!" she panted. "Come back!"

Ollie was already on the main road, her leg thrown over the bike's saddle. She rode home as fast as she could, bent low over her handlebars, hair streaming in the wind, the book lying in her pocket like a secret.

3

OLIVIA ADLER'S HOUSE was tall and lupine-purple and old. Her dad had bought the house before he and Mom had ever met. The first time Ollie's mom saw it, she said to Ollie's dad, "Who *are* you, the Easter Bunny?" because her dad had painted the house the colors of an Easter egg, and ever since, they'd called the house the Egg. The outside had plum-colored trim and a bright red door. The kitchen was green, like mint ice cream. The bedrooms were sunset-orange and candy-pink and fire-red. Dad liked colors. "Why have a gray kitchen if you can have a green one?" he would ask.

Ollie loved her house. When her grandparents visited, they would always shake their heads and say how white walls really opened up a place. Dad would nod agreeably, and then wink at Ollie when Grandma wasn't looking.

Mom had given the rooms names.

"Dawn Room," Ollie remembered her mother saying, holding her hand and walking her through the house, waiting while Ollie's stumpy legs climbed the stairs. Ollie must have just been learning to read, because she remembered looking up at the sign on each door and trying to sound out the words: "*D-a-w-n*. Dawn." Her mother's hand was warm and strong, callused from climbing and paddling. Ollie could still remember her small fat fingers secure in her mother's thin brown ones.

"That means when the sun comes up, Olivia."

Ollie's mom was the only one who called her *Olivia*. "If you have a brother, we're going to name him Sebastian. Two beautiful names. Why make them shorter?"

Ms. Carruthers had tried to call Ollie *Olivia* at the end of fifth grade, and a few teachers had tried since, but Ollie refused to answer. All the best heroines of Ollie's books were stubborn as rocks, or roots, or whatever the author liked to call them. Only her mom called her Olivia and that was that.

"Dusk Room," Ollie's mother said, tilting the sign on the door so Ollie could see. She and Dad had painted the signs themselves. Dad's were perfect, with suns and moons and tiny flowers. Dad was crafty; he painted and knitted hats and baked. Ollie's mom liked digging in the dirt and running and flying and adventurous things. Her signs were exuberant blobs of paint in which the letters were barely visible.

"Dusk means when the sun goes down!" Ollie's voice piped in delighted reply.

"And this one?" said Ollie's mother at the end of the hallway. The door to this room had an old-fashioned keyhole and a doorknob shaped like a dragon.

"Your mother found that doorknob in some yard sale," her dad told Ollie once. "She had to have it. 'For my daughter,' she said."

"Ollie's room!" Ollie cried triumphantly. Her mother had laughed and scooped her up and run with her upsidedown all the way back to the kitchen.

———

Ollie had to pass the Brewsters' house on her way home. During the day, the skeleton in their attic looked silly, but now, at dusk, it looked sinister. Its lit-up green eyes seemed to follow her. The witch on the front porch grinned and cackled. Ollie hurried past, trying not to look over her shoulder.

Just a crazy person. I just met a crazy person. That's all. That doesn't mean I have to be scared of everything now, come on . . .

And stole something from a crazy person, another part of her replied. *They put people in the slammer for stealing stuff. Juvenile detention. You'll have to graduate high school in prison pajamas.*

It was easier thinking that than the other thought. *What if she knocks on the door at midnight, with that same look in her eyes, wanting the book back?*

Ollie heaved her bike into the toolshed and clattered through the front door. The streaky shadows on the lawn seemed to chase her indoors. The weather was changing; the wind that had rattled the leaves by the swimming hole was now tearing down the mountain, swinging arcs of sunset shadows across the Egg. Rain began to spatter the driveway. The warm weather was over.

But inside the Egg, everything was bright and normal. Ollie hung her jacket on its peg, pocket heavy with the weight of her prize. She reached for the book, then thought better of it. If she didn't show it to anyone, she could always *deny* taking it. Would anyone believe her?

Would they believe the woman by the river?

Her dad was in the kitchen. Simon and Garfunkel crooned on the speakers, accompanied by the clanking of pots. Over the music her dad called, "That you, Ollie?"

"Nope," said Ollie, still a little shaky. "It's the postman. Someone just sent me a puppy, a kitten, and a pony for my birthday."

"Great," came her dad's voice from the kitchen. "The pony can mow the lawn, and I will personally feed the kitten to Mrs. Who." Dad didn't like cats. Mrs. Who was the great horned owl that lived in the dead hickory tree at the far corner of their yard. "But you can keep the puppy," her dad added with an air of generosity. "Although I thought your birthday was in April."

"Ha-ha," said Ollie. She crossed the slate floor of the entryway, edged around the piano, stepped into the living room. As she did, some of that afternoon's weirdness started to lose its grip.

Ollie's dad sold people solar panels. He liked it fine. But what he really loved was making things. Ollie had never seen his hands still, not since she was a baby. In the long summer afternoons, he built birdhouses or furniture; in the evenings he cooked or knitted or showed her how to make plates out of clay.

That evening, her dad was baking. The whole house smelled like bread. Ollie sniffed. Garlic bread. There was tomato sauce. And Dad, seeing her come in, had just dumped a pile of noodles into a pot of boiling water. Spaghetti. Great. She was starving.

The living room and the kitchen were one big space, with a kitchen island separating them. Ollie dropped her backpack and threw herself backward over the couch.

Ollie's dad stood behind the kitchen island, stirring, humming along with the music. His shirt was long sleeved and mustard colored. Dad liked colors on clothes like he liked colors on houses—the brighter the better. Sometimes they didn't go together. Mom teased him for it.

Ordinarily her dad would have handed her a piece of garlic bread and while Ollie ate it, they would have argued over her drinking a ginger ale before dinner, and by the time she'd worn him down, the pasta would have been ready, and it wouldn't be *before dinner* anymore. But now her dad's expression had turned serious and the garlic bread stayed in the oven. Ollie thought about staging an oven raid and then thought better of it.

She surveyed her dad upside down. It was possible the school hadn't called.

Her dad pressed pause on Simon and Garfunkel. "Ollie."

"The school called," said Ollie.

"Brian Battersby's mother called me first," said her dad. He couldn't maintain angry-dad voice even when he was trying; now he just sounded exasperated. "I got an earful, let me tell you. And *then* the school called. You have to go to the principal tomorrow. Ollie, you could have really hurt that boy."

"No, I couldn't!" said Ollie, sitting up. "It was only a tiny rock. Besides, they were being mean to Coco Zintner. *You* always tell me I should stick up for people."

Her dad quit stirring the sauce and came and sat down beside her. Now he was going to be understanding. She hated understanding voice as much as she hated sympathy face. Ollie felt her ears start to burn.

"Ollie," he said. "I'm really glad you were trying to help someone. But don't try that innocent face with me. There's about a million ways to help a friend out without giving anyone stitches, as you know perfectly well. I don't care if Brian was being a little turd. Next time get a teacher, use *words*, blind 'em with mathematics; God, use that imagination of yours." He knocked playfully on Ollie's forehead. "First thing tomorrow morning at the principal's office, young lady. You're going to be in detention for a while if Brian's mother has anything to say about it." He paused, added mildly, "Brian is fine, by the way. His mother seemed to think he wasn't taking the incident as seriously as he should be."

"Of course he's not. His head's about seven inches thick," grumbled Ollie. "I could have thrown a brick and he'd be fine."

"Please don't," said her dad. "As the caterpillar said to the blackbird. Also, Coco Zintner's mother called. Coco says thanks for standing up to them. Apparently, no one else did."

Ollie said nothing. She felt bad now about hitting Brian in the head with a rock, and also bad because she didn't really *like* Coco Zintner. Coco squeaked too much. Ollie just didn't like watching someone get teased. She was also hungry, and she wanted to tell her dad about the woman beside the swimming hole, but it didn't seem like the time. She did *not* want to be in detention until Christmas.

Well, Ollie thought, *if they put me in jail for stealing a book, I won't be.* But that was hardly better. Out of the frying pan and into the fire.

"If you want to throw things," her dad said gently, "why not rejoin the softball team? They'd take you back in a heartbeat, I know, slugger. Remember your home run last—"

She stiffened. "Don't want to."

Her dad stood up. He didn't look mad or exasperated. He just looked hurt, which was worst of all.

"'Kay, fine," he said, heading back toward the stove. "You don't have to. But, Ollie, you can't hide in your books forever. There are all kinds of people, and good things, and life, just waiting for you to—"

She had known he was going to say that, or something like that. She was on her feet. "To what? Forget? I won't, even if you have. I'll do what I want. You are not the boss of me."

"I am the dad of you," her dad pointed out. He had gone pale under his beard. "I'm trying to help, kiddo. I'm sad still too, you know, but I—"

She didn't want to hear it. Of all the things in the world, it was the last thing she wanted to hear. "I'm not hungry," said Ollie. "I'm going to bed."

"Ollie—"

"*Not hungry.*"

She grabbed her backpack, made for the stairs, in the entryway, scooped up her prize from the swimming hole in passing. The stairs were steep, the hallway to her room long and full of shadows. She sped down it.

Part of her wanted her dad to follow her, tell her she was being silly. She wanted him to crack a dumb joke and coax her downstairs to dinner. But only silence chased her up the stairs to her room.

Ollie didn't slam the door. No, she'd already had her tantrum. To slam the door would be too obvious. Make her an angry kid (*which you are, dummy*) instead of an angry almost-teenager who Had the Right to Be Mad.

So Ollie gritted her teeth and closed her door very softly. Then, where no one could see, she threw herself onto her comforter and buried her face in her pillow. She didn't cry. She squeezed her eyes shut but she didn't cry. It wasn't something she had tears for, anyway. Tears were for things like skinning your knee, not for . . .

Whatever. Ollie just got mad sometimes, and people talking to her made it worse. It was easier to be by herself, up here where it was quiet. Even though she *was* hungry. She could still smell garlic. But her dad would want to talk more and Ollie didn't have any words for him.

Or maybe he'd let her be quiet. Sometimes he did. But in its way, silence between them was worse. Better to stay up here.

Ollie dug a russet apple out of her bag. Evansburg had the best apples. It was harvest time and the market was full of fresh cider and every type of apple in the world. Red and purple and yellow and green apples. *Crunch.* Ollie bit down. Apples were good. She would think about apples. Ollie practically lived on apples in October. She tried to convince herself that an apple was as good as pasta. Fail. But it was something. She'd sneak down later for a proper snack. Snacks. She thought about snacks.

Not enough. She needed a better distraction. Distractions were good. Then she wouldn't have to think of her dad, pale under his beard. She wouldn't have to think of Mr. Easton and his too-sympathetic face. She wouldn't have to think about fire in a torn-up field beneath the rain. She wouldn't have to think at all.

Ollie had dropped her backpack on the rug and tossed the old book onto the desk when she first came in. Now she got off her bed and wandered over to examine it. The book had a worn-out cloth cover with its title stamped in faded gold letters. It was very thin, less than a hundred pages. Ollie picked it up.

Small Spaces. No author. Just the title.

Ollie opened the book, scanned the copyright page.

1895. *Wow*, Ollie thought. *Super old*. Printed in Boston. Ollie turned the page.

It started with a letter.

My Dearest Margaret,

I wish I could have told you this story in person. More than anything, I wish I had one more hour, one more day, a little more time.

Ollie bit her lip. She too had wished for more time. She sank down on her bed, reading, chewing her apple without really noticing.

> *But I don't. This—these words are all I have.*
>
> *I know you have often wondered why I do not speak of your father. I am going to tell you why. I do not know if you will believe me. Set down in black and white, I barely believe these words myself.*
>
> *But I promise you that everything I say in here is true.*
>
> *Once you have read, I hope you will forget. The farm is yours now. Sell it, if you can. Above all, I beg you to leave the past alone. Think of the future. Think of your family.*
>
> *Do not go back to Smoke Hollow. The twilights when the mist rises—the dangerous nights—get more frequent as the year draws to a close. Jonathan told me that. Before he . . . well. I will come to that.*
>
> *I can't tell you how I have thought of leaving this place. I meant to, you know. Your father and I even talked of it. But he said the curse was his alone, and he could not escape it. I would not leave him.*
>
> *Now he is gone.*

There—the candle is guttering. Lights flicker,
you know, when they are near. Sometimes I hope
desperately that Jonathan is with them. That he has
never left me at all. But mostly I hope he is safely
dead, and that I will see him in the next world.
Because the alternative is so much worse.
God bless you, my dear. Even if this story
seems strange, I beg you will read it. For my sake.

With all my love,
Beth Webster, née Bouvier
Smoke Hollow, 1895

Ollie turned the page, fascinated. The next page only had an epigraph:

When the mist rises, and the smiling man comes walking,
you must avoid large places at night.
Keep to small.

Ollie frowned.

Small spaces, said the woman by the creek.

Well, the woman was obviously not right in the head; maybe the book had set her off somehow? Ollie eyed the epigraph with puzzlement. The rain tapped against her skylight; the wind was working up a temper outside. Ollie turned another page.

I was born just after the end of the war. And I was a child in 1876 when Jonathan and Caleb and their mother, Cathy Webster, came to Smoke Hollow. They were all dusty, the boys barefoot, wearing patchwork shirts. Between the three of them, they had nothing but a little bread and smoked ham tied up in a napkin.

They walked past the farm gate, past the hog pens and the chicken coop. When they got to the barnyard, the first thing they saw was me, as I was then. A pig-tailed girl, wearing brown calico, red-faced from the oven and holding a pie dish.

"Mister," I said to Jonathan. "Pop's in the north field."

Jonathan was fourteen then: nearly a man in my eyes. But he grinned at me, like we'd known each other forever.

"We'll wait," Jonathan said cheerfully. "I was hoping your pop was hiring."

4

OLLIE'S ALARM WENT off way too early the next day. She poked her bleary head out from under the covers, heard the rain rattling the roof, said, "Nope," and pulled her head back in. *Small Spaces* lay, bookmarked, within arm's reach. Ollie had stayed up late reading. She wished she'd just read all night. After she finally went to sleep, she woke up twice from the same nightmare: gray skies and burning grass and trying frantically to run to someone she couldn't see, while an endless stream of giant people holding casseroles crowded around her, saying, *I'm so sorry, Olivia.*

It was still raining. Ollie's bedroom ceiling sloped down low over her bed. Sometimes when it poured, she would pretend she was lying in a jungle waterfall. But now Ollie kept herself tucked in her blankets.

"Ollie!" her dad bellowed from the foot of the stairs. "Don't even think about that snooze button! Rain boots, extra sweater, brush your teeth, and get down here now! You're going to the farm, remember?"

A large stuffed rabbit, eyeless and noseless, lay face-to-face with Ollie. She glared at it. *"Today?* Maybe I should hope for detention."

The rain roared down, as though in agreement.

Their whole class was going to Misty Valley Farm; no little downpour would stop Mr. Easton. He'd been talking it up for weeks. They were going to learn about milking cows and slaughtering hogs (cut the throat and then hang it up to drain!) and growing broccoli (the yummiest flower). It was supposed to make them appreciate Vermont's agricultural history. Ollie looked out her skylight and was sure of only one thing: it would make them get wet.

Very quietly, as though her father downstairs would hear, Ollie stuck an arm out from under her comforter, reached for *Small Spaces*, and pulled it under the blanket with her. The first part of the book was all about Beth's childhood with Caleb and Jonathan. There was a lot of haying and pie-baking and lambing and fishing. Ollie had been delighted, but it didn't really explain why the woman by the creek was trying to throw the book away.

But now Beth's tone had changed.

Dearest, I have told you a little of my youth. Forgive an old woman's rambling. I wished to set it all down so

31

that I could live it again, and so that you could remember the good times you did not see. But now I must tell you the rest.

Jonathan told me this part of the story himself. It may seem unbelievable. You may judge for yourself. But I believe him. Listen now, but do not condemn your father. He meant well.

I have told you of our delightful childhood years, after my father hired Caleb and Jonathan and Cathy and gave them a home at Smoke Hollow. The boys were my dearest friends, and Cathy was like a second mother.

But when I was seventeen, my father died. Suddenly I was no longer a child. I was a woman with a farm to manage. Overnight it seemed that Caleb and Jonathan weren't just my childhood friends anymore. They began vying for my attention, and eventually to grow suspicious of each other. I am afraid I did little to prevent them. I was an heiress, you know, and they loved me. I—I rather liked them fighting for my time. It was like knights-errant, I thought. I was young and foolish.

Of course, I had always known which brother I wanted to marry. I had known since Jonathan smiled at me, the day I met him. When Jonathan asked for my hand, I said yes.

Caleb was furious when he found out. The two brothers quarreled. Jon wouldn't tell me all that they

32

said, but I gather that some of the insults on both sides were unforgivable. The night they argued, there was a storm up. You remember how Smoke Hollow gets when it storms in October. There was ice on the rocks by Lethe Creek; freezing rain poured down. The brothers' shouting came to blows. Jonathan struck his brother. Caleb, weeping, ran outside alone.

Jonathan, still angry, decided it best to let Caleb go. He would get cold, Jonathan reasoned, and come back.

But Caleb didn't come back.

One day, two days, and Caleb didn't come back. Search parties were sent out. They found no trace of him. Their mother, Cathy, frantic, blamed Jonathan for Caleb's disappearance. Grief made her wild. One night, she and Jonathan fought in turn. Cathy must have been half mad with sadness and shock by then. She told Jon to leave her house and not return until he had brought back his brother.

Jonathan was eaten up with guilt. When his mother ordered him to go out, he went. It was raining, he told me later. Very softly: a rain like cold tears. The mist was rising with the rain, the mist that gives Smoke Hollow its name. It was nearly Samhain, which, in the Old Country, marked the turning of the year.

I cannot excuse what he did next. But Jon was desperate, outside in the wet, grieving. "Please," Jonathan

said aloud. "Please. I'm sorry. I just want him back. I'll
do anything. Anything."

And, out of the mist, a voice answered—

"Are you reading?" Dad bellowed from below. Ollie popped her head out of the covers with a jerk. "Put it down. I want to hear footsteps! Clothes! Boots! Coat! Now!" And then he added, in a coaxing sort of bellow, "I made bacon and oatmeal! I *know* you're hungry."

She was. She had skipped both dinner and snacks the night before. The smell of bacon drifted deliciously up the stairs. What she *really* wanted was to eat bacon and oatmeal in bed, and to finish *Small Spaces*. Putting a quiver in her voice, Ollie called, "I think I have a fever." She pressed an experimental hand to her forehead. Definitely warm. "I shouldn't go out in the rain," she added. "I might catch pneumonia."

Ollie heard her dad's footsteps. She managed to shove her book under the covers, huddle down into the blankets, and assume a pathetic expression a second before he walked in.

Ollie's dad wore blue plaid. He looked as though he hadn't slept at all; he was rumpled, and a splotch of oatmeal was stuck to his shirt. His fingers fidgeted, as though looking for something to do. At first he seemed worried, then his look turned to exasperation.

"Yep, you do look sick," her dad said. "Very sick.

Nothing to do but to stay here with some tea and dry toast." He pounced on the book, which was just peeking out from under her blanket. Ollie winced. "No books, of course," he added. "Too much excitement might give you the flu."

Ollie looked from her dad to the book. A day alone in bed with dry toast? At least she could read on the bus.

She coughed once, bravely. "I am feeling a little better." She tried out a noble expression. "I don't want to get behind in school."

"How brave of you," said her dad.

Ollie got out of her bed, with dignity.

"Five minutes," said her father, bounding back down to the kitchen, from which drifted the smell of now-burning bacon.

Ollie looked up at her skylight. The rain slanted across the glass. It was like looking into an aquarium. Maybe, Ollie thought, they all really lived underwater, like merpeople, but didn't know it, because to them water was just like air.

No, that was silly. The cool air of her room was punishment after her warm covers. She shoved her feet into fuzzy slippers and stumbled, shivering, to her dresser.

After some consideration, Ollie put on faded jeans, a long green sweater, and woolly socks her dad had knitted with a fish on one and a fisherman on the other. Her yellow rain boots were waiting for her downstairs by the back door.

She reached under her pillow for a big black wristwatch with a cracked face and put this on carefully. She didn't bother to comb her hair. Combs just made her curls frizz. Finally, she stepped back, scowled at her reflection, went to the bathroom, hastily brushed her teeth, shoved *Small Spaces* into her backpack, and padded down the stairs.

Ollie didn't make a lot of noise in her socks, but when she stepped into the kitchen, her dad still turned around right away. In some ways, he hadn't changed much since last year. He told jokes and knitted socks just like he always had. But his thick, dark hair had silver threads that hadn't been there before, and sometimes Ollie would catch him staring blankly into space when he thought she wasn't looking.

"Look at your dad's eyes," her mom had said once, when all three of them were paddling down the Connecticut River. Ollie was sitting in the middle of the canoe and her dad was behind her in the stern. From the bow, Ollie's mom looked back and smiled, her nose sunburned red. "Aren't your dad's eyes the loveliest in the whole world?" They were: big and velvety. So dark that you couldn't see where the colored part ended and the pupil began. "You have just the same eyes, Olivia, my heartbreaker."

Ollie had smiled and her dad had laughed and said, "You've got my eyes, maybe, Ollie-pop, but you're as brave as your mother."

Standing in the kitchen, Ollie shook the memory away. Her dad had gotten Bernie, the woodstove, going. The fire crackled and pinged behind the stove's glass door. The hallway and the stairs had been cold, but the kitchen was warm.

A big pot of oatmeal steamed on the stove and three nice crackly-brown loaves sat on the counter. Dad must have kept on baking after the garlic bread. Maybe he'd baked all night, waiting for Ollie to come down.

Ollie decided not to think about that. She wasn't going to feel *bad* about that. Think about breakfast. Toast? Ollie decided on oatmeal. She got herself a bowl, crumbled bacon into the oatmeal, then dumped a lot of cream and maple syrup on top. Ollie had helped tap the trees for syrup herself, the winter before. This was the last batch of syrup they had all made together: Mom and her tapping and her dad keeping the big pot boiling for days on end.

Don't think about that either. Ollie put her oatmeal on the kitchen island and went to pour herself some coffee.

"You're too young for coffee," said her dad, not looking up. He was sitting at the kitchen table and scrolling through the news.

"I'm not too young to go out in the rain and catch pneumonia," said Ollie, pouring herself a cup anyway and stirring in sugar.

Her dad looked up. He wasn't eating his own oatmeal.

"Take more oatmeal, then," he said, catching sight of her bowl. "There are raisins and walnuts in the jars on the spice shelf. You must be starving. You didn't come down last night."

He *had* waited up.

Ollie definitely felt bad now. Guiltily—and also because she *was* really hungry—Ollie added some raisins and a pat of butter to her oatmeal, and gave the whole mess a stir.

"Ready for the farm today?" her dad said. Just yesterday, "I was talking about Misty Valley with Mr. Brewster. Linda Webster's only been in business for five years, but she's really doing well for herself. The farm's revitalized the county. I'm a bit jealous you get to see it all firsthand. Think I could join the sixth grade and come along?"

"Only if you've been practicing your drowned-rat impressions," said Ollie, with a dark look at the streaming window. She added warm milk to her coffee and brought her mug and her refreshed bowl of oatmeal back to the table.

Her dad snorted and glanced at the rain sluicing down the windows. "There is that. Bring a hat. I'll have the stove going when you get back."

"Hot chocolate?" Ollie suggested.

"With marshmallows," said her dad, and smiled a smile that went all the way to the crinkles on either side of his eyes. It was a smile she didn't see very much anymore.

Ollie almost smiled back. Maybe getting wet wouldn't be so bad. She took a big sip of her coffee and opened *Small*

Spaces. She could feel her dad watching her over her book, but she didn't look. Looking would make her feel guilty all over again. Ollie forced her attention to her book.

White mist crept up from the creek. Softly it slipped toward Jonathan, standing tearstained in the rain.

A man walked out of the smoky dark.

"What did he look like?" I asked Jonathan later.

"He smiled," Jonathan told me. "He didn't tell me his name. I don't think he has a name. He had long fingers. Long, thin fingers, and, oh, I can't remember the rest. I felt as though I'd known him since the day I was born, and I felt the most indescribable horror at the sight of him."

When the man spoke, his voice was gentle. "I think you called me," he said to Jonathan, while the rain streamed around them.

"No," said Jonathan. "I called my brother."

"Your brother is gone," said the man. "But I could bring him back for you." He smiled. "For a price."

Jonathan's knees shook. But he still stammered, "Wh-what price?"

"When I ask, you will come with me and do as I say," said the man. "If you do, you will have your brother back again."

"For how long?" Jonathan asked. "How long would I have to do as you say?"

The man's smile broadened. His eyes were dark as a river at midnight. "Until the mist turns to rain," he said.

"Ollie. Ollie!"

Ollie took a deep breath, blinking in the cozy, firelit kitchen. She had thought it was dark as a rainy night on an old farm.

Her dad looked from her to the book. "Were you not listening at all? I was giving you such a fantastic speech too."

"Speech?" said Ollie, still dazed.

"Yep," said her dad. "The 'Be good today, stay dry, I love you' speech. It's in the manual somewhere."

Ollie just blinked at him.

Her dad sighed. "'Kay," he said. "How about this instead?" He thought for a minute. "What did the frog say about the book?"

"Dunno," Ollie said distractedly, still thinking about *Small Spaces*.

"Reddit," said her dad, making frog noises. "Reddit."

Ollie groaned.

"And then what did the *chicken* say?" asked her dad, looking pleased with himself.

Ollie put her head in her hands.

"Book book book booook!" said her dad, making clucking sounds.

Ollie cracked a tiny smile.

"Come on," her dad said, taking a last swig of coffee. "I'll drive you. Hurry."

Ollie finished her own coffee, swiped her spoon through the last of her oatmeal, and followed her dad into the rain.

5

BEN WITHERS MIDDLE SCHOOL always looked shabby, its paint peeling around the windows, its roof drooping in. But today, under the gray sky, the school looked sad and lonely. It lay curled up behind its fence like a huge stray dog. Ollie imagined that the building was actually a giant dog. It would come to life and be Ollie's friend and they would go on adventures...

Her dad drove into the parking lot, bouncing over potholes. The car shuddered to a halt, and Ollie's daydream disappeared. She hunched in the passenger seat, one finger holding her place in her book.

"Can't you leave that with me?" asked her father hopefully. "You might try talking on the bus instead. Jenna misses you—and I know Coco Zintner wants to be your friend—"

Something in Ollie's face silenced him.

"Jenna just wants to talk about how she feels *bad* for

me. *Still.* I hate it. Coco's from the city and just silly." Ollie pointed to her book. "I think Jonathan might have just sold his soul to the smiling man!"

"Well," muttered her dad, "it was worth a try."

Ollie picked up her polka-dot backpack and grabbed the door handle.

"Look, Ollie . . ." said her dad.

She waited.

Her dad sighed, and changed whatever he'd been about to say. "Okay, how about this one? What's the difference between a cat and a comma?"

"Dad—"

"Well?"

"I don't know, what?"

Her dad grinned. "A comma," he informed her, "is a pause at the end of a clause."

Ollie saw where this was going. "*Dad.*"

"But a *cat*," her dad finished blithely, "has *claws* at the ends of its *paws.*"

He busted up laughing and Ollie snorted despite herself. "That was better than usual." She slouched out of the car.

"Oh wait, I forgot. Here," said her dad. He reached into the back seat and thrust her lunch box out the window. Ollie undid the clasps and peered into the depths. Carrot sticks and peanut butter cookies—way too many of both—and a very large turkey sandwich, cut in quarters, on homemade bread. Maple granola, with sugared walnuts. A chocolate chip muffin. Dad really must have baked all night.

"I'm too old to pack a lunch," Ollie said, but not very convincingly. The muffin looked fantastic. "They'll have lunch at the farm. *And* I think someone is supposed to bring donuts to homeroom this morning."

"Pah, donuts," said her dad. "That's not food, that's like anti-food."

Ollie was fond of cake donuts. "They're totally food."

"Come on," said her dad, abandoning that argument. "Take it anyway. You never know. You might get hungry!"

Her dad was smiling. But his eyes were dark and a little sad: *Please, Ollie, I made it for you, come on,* and so she took the lunch box and stuck it hastily into her backpack. "Thanks, Dad," she said. Her lunch box was pale blue, with a pink unicorn on the front. She had loved it when she was younger. Her dad refused to hear her hints about switching to paper sacks.

"Love you, Ollie-pop!" he called as she strode away, loud enough for the entire town, let alone the middle school, to hear.

———

Ollie had her hand on the front door when she remembered that she had to go to the principal's office. Gah.

Principal Snyder's office was down a long hallway. The

hallway had green walls, not so nice a shade as Ollie's kitchen, and green-and-brown-freckled linoleum. The office door had a large WELCOME sign on it, with a worm waving from a hole in an apple.

Ollie disliked this sign. One of her dad's jokes went, "What's worse than finding a worm in an apple? . . . Finding *half* a worm in an apple." Ollie had found both worms and half worms in apples before. Most kids from Evansburg had.

Thinking of apples, Ollie went in.

The first person she saw was Brian Battersby, looking helpful and sincere. It was not an expression that sat naturally on his face, in Ollie's opinion. He spent too much time acting cool.

The next person she saw was Principal Snyder, looking frustrated. "Now, Brian," she said, "tell me again what happened."

"I tripped," said Brian cheerfully. "Bad luck."

Ollie stared at him. Was Brian—*covering* for her?

"Ollie," said Principal Snyder, turning gravely to her.

"Um, yes?" said Ollie. "That's me. Ollie here." She waved.

"Did you throw a rock?" said Principal Snyder. "Yesterday? Did you hit Brian with a rock outside the school building?"

Behind Principal Snyder, Brian shook his head at Ollie.

"Um, maybe?" said Ollie, not sure how Brian wanted

her to play this. "I did a lot of things yesterday. I do most days, you know, with the school and the home and—"

"Anyone could have done it," Brian put in. "No harm, no foul."

"It cut you in the head!" cried Principal Snyder.

"Accidentally," said Brian, and he added, with unexpected crispness, "You can't pursue justice on my behalf if I don't choose to have it pursued. I'm the star witness."

Ollie gaped at Brian but hastily arranged her face to vigorous agreement when Principal Snyder looked her way.

The principal rubbed her temples, looking from Ollie to Bryan. "I can't have students injuring other students," she said.

"Just an accident," said Brian. "Besides, it probably wasn't her. If there was a rock, I definitely didn't see her throw it."

"Of course you didn't see her!" said the principal. "She hit you on the back of the head, therefore she was standing behind you!"

Neither of them said anything. Principal Snyder looked again from Ollie to Brian. Ollie thought of Coco Zintner and tried to look angelic.

Maybe it worked. Abruptly Principal Snyder's face softened. Sympathy face. Ollie almost let her innocent expression slip. She *hated* sympathy face.

"Well, it is chivalrous of you, Brian," said the principal.

Ollie bristled. Implying that Brian was only sticking up

for her (*Why was he sticking up for her?*) because she was a *girl*: that was dumb. Or worse, it was because Ollie was *that girl*. But she bit her tongue. Whatever Brian was doing, it was working.

"Make sure it doesn't happen again," said the principal, misty-eyed now. "I'm *so* glad to see you making new friends, Ollie. Run along, you two."

Ollie and Brian burst together out of Principal Snyder's office, and the second the door banged shut behind them, Ollie turned to Brian and said, in a voice dripping scorn, "*Chivalrous?*"

Brian looked lofty. "I didn't want to get a girl in trouble. You could say thanks, you know. I just got you out of detention until Christmas."

"First of all, I got *myself* in trouble," Ollie said. "I don't need you to get me in trouble, thank you very much. And don't treat me special because I'm a girl. That's sexist."

"Being nice to you is sexist?"

"If you're being nice just 'cause I'm a girl, it is!"

"I didn't even say *chivalrous*; that was Principal Snyder! Besides, can we focus on the part where I just got you out of detention?" Brian had been looking proud of himself; now he looked a little deflated.

"You could have just stuck up for Coco. Then I wouldn't have been in the principal's office in the first place. Where was your *chivalry* then?"

"I couldn't stick up for Coco," said Brian in a reasonable tone. "Then people might think I liked her back."

They were hustling down the hall; the bell was about to ring.

"Who cares what people think?" Ollie demanded. She was a little out of breath, trying to walk faster than him, but Brian just glided along beside her, hands in his pockets, acting as though he weren't in a hurry to get to class at all.

"I care," said Brian.

"Where'd you even learn to talk like that, anyway? *Star witness.*"

"*Law & Order,*" said Brian at once. "My mom's a fan. You still haven't said thank you."

"Because I—" Ollie began hotly, then stopped. Brian stopped too, weirdly. Why didn't he say have a nice day and go away? Worse, he was still talking.

"You know, Ollie," he said, "that was a really good throw. With the rock." He made a rock-throwing gesture. "You were like twenty meters away." Brian was born in Jamaica; his parents had moved up to Evansburg to open a spa when he was a toddler. You wouldn't know where he was from by talking to him, except that sometimes he said *irie* instead of *good* or used *meters* instead of *feet*. Also he was black, which was notable in small-town Vermont. "Then it was just like *wham*—"

But Ollie had stopped listening. She had paused at a

window that looked out at the old hickory tree and beyond it to the muddy soccer field. The rain hurried down, sleek and silver, the kind of rain that seems to gather mist as it falls and fill the air with water. It had been raining that day last January, a weird, unseasonable, smoky rain: rain that washed away snow and iced up engines. It had been raining that day when her dad came to school, and just there under that tree he had said . . .

"Never mind," she said. "The bell's about to ring."

With that she hurried off, leaving Brian puzzled behind her.

6

THE CLASS WANDERED IN, or sprinted in just as the bell rang, to find the promised donuts nestled in a white box at the front of the room. Mr. Easton knew the value of food bribes, especially on a cold, wet Farm Day.

Ollie took a plain cake donut. She would save her chocolate chip muffin for later. Munching, she stowed her stuff and pulled out *Small Spaces*. She'd just read for a minute.

> *The next day, Caleb came back.*
>
> *He was pale and blue-lipped; his eyes were strange and distant. I remember thinking, with a shiver, that a drowned man breathed back to life would look like him. But it was really him. It was his voice, his smile. Only the look in his eyes had changed, and he would not say where he had been. "I don't remember," he said. The town*

*decided that he must have hit his head and wandered for
days insensible. I made myself believe it too.*

*I have never seen anyone so glad as Cathy was
when her two sons came back to her. She cried with joy
and didn't even notice the look in Caleb's eyes.*

The next pages dealt with Beth's wedding, the honey-
moon. Ollie began to skim. She wanted to know the end;
she wanted to know what had happened with the smiling
man. She caught snatches along the way.

*Caleb was best man at the wedding, standing silent at
his brother's side. Cathy cried again when we said our
vows. She loved her sons very much.*

*We were a month in France after the wedding, and I
did not think the Mediterranean was as beautiful as
Smoke Hollow in spring.*

The night you were born, it snowed in May.

*I have never loved anyone so much as I loved my Jona-
than, except for you, dearest daughter. There was so
much joy—so much peace in our house.*

Until one night.

Ollie began reading properly again.

It was autumn. There had been cold rain all the day,

and the mist was rising in the corn. It was just after the harvest, and the stalks rustled, gray and dead. Jonathan had been out late. In the barn, I thought. One of the cows was calving out of season.

Jonathan came in, wet, his hair plastered down. He didn't smell like the barn, not at all. His eyes were white-rimmed, wild.

"He came back, Beth my girl," he said, sank into a chair near the woodstove and buried his face in his hands. "The smiling man came back."

"I *said*," Mr. Easton's voice broke in, "what is the significance of Misty Valley Farm, Ollie?"

Ollie looked up, a little wild-eyed herself. Oh, right. Class must have started, and she hadn't noticed. Well, it wasn't the first time. Ollie's shoulders stiffened; she took a bite of donut and said, without missing a beat, "Misty Valley Farm is the best example in the state of Vermont of the possibilities achievable in small-scale farming." Giggles swept the room; she was imitating Mr. Easton in lecture mode. Ollie thought she heard Mr. Easton sigh.

"The farm has had tremendous success cultivating corn and wheat, along with apple, plum, and pear orchards," Ollie continued. "They also run an extensive dairy operation and side businesses in local florals and sugaring. During harvest time, they are one of the biggest employers in the county."

Ollie remembered nearly everything she read, a vital talent for any girl who reads novels in class and doesn't pay attention. Having neatly recited the introduction to Misty Valley from its website, Ollie tried to find her place again in her book. Without looking up, she could feel the words trembling on Mr. Easton's tongue. *What is that you're reading, Ollie? Now is not the time for novels. Put it away.*

But—sympathy face again. Also, Ollie *had* answered his question. When Coco Zintner's hand shot into the air, Mr. Easton only said mildly, "That is correct, Ollie," and turned to Coco. Ollie wished she hadn't made fun of him.

"Do you have something to add, Miss Zintner?"

Coco evidently did. She was half out of her seat, waving her hand. You had to hand it to Coco. Anyone else would have crept into class, head down, hoping the notebook incident had been forgotten. Not Coco Zintner. "Um," said Coco, the words tumbling out, "I just have a question. What about the ghosts?"

A faint murmur of interest ran through the room.

"My mom told me about them," Coco added smugly. Coco's mom was a reporter for the *Evansburg Independent*. She had come to talk to their class once, casual in her jeans, with a thick, ash-colored ponytail. She made Mr. Easton go giggly. "Can you tell us, please?"

Mr. Easton looked torn. "I wouldn't say there are

ghosts," he said. "Not exactly. But there are certainly some sad episodes in Misty Valley's past."

Sad episodes were more interesting than agriculture. "Tell us!" said Phil Greenblatt, and the rest of the class took up the cry. Coco looked proud of herself.

Mr. Easton hesitated. He probably liked talking about ghosts too.

"Well, Misty Valley has been a farm for a while," said Mr. Easton, giving in. "Or at least, people have been farming that land a long time. Back in the 1800s, it was called—oh, foggy—smoky—something. I forget now. It gets foggy after dark because of humidity off the river. That's why it's called Misty Valley now."

Ollie thought of the smiling man, coming out of the smoky dark.

"There were two brothers who worked in the fields," said Mr. Easton. "They used to go about with the owner's daughter. The girl wasn't even eighteen when her father died and she became the owner herself. Both boys were in love with her, and there was a lot of talk in Evansburg. Folk wondering which brother she would marry. Fifty acres isn't anything to sneeze at."

Ollie frowned and glanced at her book.

"She married the older brother, in the end. If his younger brother was jealous, there's no record of it. They all lived on the farm. The married couple had at least one kid, a girl. The girl grew up, got married herself, moved away. All normal, right?"

There were probably lots of brothers trying to marry the same farm girl in the nineteenth century, Ollie thought, but she looked at her book again.

The whole class shifted in their seats. Long-dead romances were not as interesting as ghosts. "But one night the older brother disappeared," Mr. Easton continued. "Just—gone. Vanished. No trace. Town rumor said the younger one had finally done him in out of jealousy."

Now the class was more interested. Ollie was listening closely. "Soon after that," Mr. Easton went on, "the *younger* brother disappeared. No one ever found traces of either of them. Eventually the sheriff decided that the younger brother had killed the elder and then been overcome with remorse and thrown himself into the creek. That was when the rumors of hauntings started. Rustling in the corn. Voices. Footsteps without feet. They said the two brothers didn't lie quiet."

Now the class was silent. In the pause, Ollie could hear the roar of rain on the school roof. She wished she knew how *Small Spaces* ended.

"The woman herself didn't live long after her husband vanished. Throughout her final illness, she swore that her husband wasn't dead, that he was still on the farm. Of course, they never found him. Legend says that now the woman haunts the farm too. Looking for her lost husband and her brother-in-law."

Eyeing the silent room, he added, "You guys good on the ghost stories?"

Phil Greenblatt poked Brian and said, "Be careful; the lady ghost might decide you're her murdered man."

Brian snorted and the strange tension broke.

"Can't imagine how your mother got hold of that story," Mr. Easton was saying to Coco. "Bit of ancient history. I suppose she talked to Linda Webster. That's how Linda got the farm, you know; she's the great—however many times great—granddaughter of that poor young woman."

Ollie stiffened. *Jonathan Webster,* Jon had said to Beth. *This is my brother, Caleb, my mother, Cathy. Beth Webster. Linda Webster.* Probably just a coincidence, though. A lot of people were named Webster.

"Websters have owned that farm since the late nineteenth century," Mr. Easton added.

The author just heard of Smoke Hollow and copied the names, thought Ollie. But sharp in her memory was a woman, her pale face makeup-smeared, her eyes darting around the sunlit swimming hole, saying *I have to.*

Coco's hand was in the air again. "That wasn't the weird thing," Coco said. "You didn't tell the bad thing. The other thing. The schoolhouse fire."

"Yes, right, okay," said Mr. Easton. He addressed the

whole class. "The Websters have *owned* the farm since the late nineteenth century. But no Websters *lived* on the farm in the twentieth century except for once, briefly. I was a boy in Evansburg at the time. A man—his name was Garrett Webster, as I recall—moved onto the old property and tried to start a back-to-nature sort of school. Basketmaking and things. It was he who renamed the farm Misty Valley. But one day, late in autumn, his schoolhouse caught fire."

The class looked at one another.

"It was right after dark. One of those thick, ugly nights. The kids had stayed late to rehearse a play, I think. The ash bucket for the woodstove caught fire, the fire department decided later. No one made it out alive. I think there's a plaque somewhere on the farm with all the names of the kids that died.

Garrett Webster moved away after that. Well, of course he did. Devastated. They said he was quite successful—became a banker or something. But he never came back. No one came back until Linda Webster."

"But the *weird* thing," insisted Coco. "You didn't say the weird thing."

"Yes, all right, Coco," said Mr. Easton patiently. "The *weird thing*, as Miss Zintner puts it, is this: they never found any bodies. The schoolhouse was burned to rubble, of course, right down to the foundation stones. People came up from Rutland to pick through it. But nothing. No bones or teeth. Nothing to bury. Just stones and the nails that had held the building together."

This didn't make any sense to Ollie. "But," she burst out, "to burn bone to ash, the fire would have had to burn at fourteen *hundred* degrees at least, for two hours or more." Ollie had done a lot of research about fires in the last year. Trying to prove to herself that there had been a way, some possible way . . . There hadn't been, of course. But she was left with useless knowledge about fires.

Mr. Easton looked pleased. Ollie had spent the last year determinedly silent in class, and here she was spouting random facts. "You aren't the first one to point that out, Ollie," said Mr. Easton. "There have been a lot of theories. Maybe the fire burned hotter than normal. Leftover heating oil, some compound in the paint. Tar.

"Those men from before," Ollie heard herself saying. "The husband and brother-in-law—they disappeared too... or maybe the children just weren't there."

"Where would they have gone?" Ollie heard herself say. "Isn't that a lot of people to just *disappear* on one farm?"

"I don't know," said Mr. Easton. "That's why they call it an unsolved mystery. The county sheriff questioned Garrett Webster pretty well, of course. A big party searched the farm grounds, thinking perhaps the fire was to cover up a crime."

At this the whole class perked up.

"They didn't find anything," said Mr. Easton, suddenly brisk, seeing the eager faces. "You gang of ghouls. Because there was nothing to find. Five years ago, Linda Webster rebuilt the old farm by the river, got it running, has been hugely successful. Now we're going there today, not to dwell on the past, but to learn more about the future of farming in this state. So can anyone tell me . . ."

Storytime was over. Ollie wished class was over. There was something in all this she didn't understand. She wanted to keep reading.

7

IT WAS STILL RAINING by the time they got done with homeroom. Ollie had listened to the announcements, with half an ear, fingers itching for her book. She could still hear Mr. Easton's voice saying *they never found any bodies.*

But Ollie didn't have time to read yet. They were going to the farm. The bell rang and the sixth grade piled outside, pulling on caps and coats and backpacks. The bus squatted in the middle of the wet parking lot like a prehistoric swamp monster, the two golden eyes of its headlights gleaming out through the fog.

Mr. Easton popped out of the bus door and the swamp-monster illusion dissolved. "Hurry up!" he shouted, waving his arm. The sixth grade hurried through the rain. Already, rows of faces peered through the bus's misted-up windows.

Ollie splashed across the puddled parking lot, cradling

her book under her rain jacket. The bus was steamy warm.

"There you are, Ollie," said Mr. Easton.

Ollie didn't answer. She was frowning at the bus driver. He was big, with a thick gray beard. In fact, he was sort of gray all over. Gray-white. Mushroom-colored. Except his lips were red. He gave her a shifting sideways grin. Ollie decided she didn't like his grin.

"Where's Ms. Hodges?" she asked. Ms. Hodges was their usual driver. She had been driving Evansburg school buses for forever. She would call students by their older siblings' names and sometimes ask Ollie, with a vaguely sympathetic tone, what she was reading.

"Resting," said this bus driver. Ollie, for no reason at all, thought of the skeleton in the Brewsters' attic lurching down the stairs. "Had to rest, did Ms. Hodges."

"*Ollie,*" said Mr. Easton. "First of all, be polite. Second of all, find a seat! It's time to go. Mr.—Jones, was it?— works on the farm. He very kindly volunteered to take over for Ms. Hodges. Such beautiful misty weather! What an adventure we'll have today, hm?"

Ollie, not being part walrus, did not like bad weather. Also, the bus driver didn't seem much like a Mr. Jones to her. But Mr. Easton was getting impatient. Ollie peered down the aisle. There were no empty seats. Except . . .

No—really?

The only empty spot was next to Brian Battersby. Well, sort of empty. Even though Brian wasn't that big, he took up most of the seat, sprawling and joking with his two friends in front of him. Why wasn't one of *them* sitting next to him? Hockey stars didn't sit by themselves.

Ollie marched down the aisle. Coco Zintner was sitting next to Monika Damron, who had headphones on and was ignoring her. Coco was scribbling in her sparkly notebook. Ollie, glancing down, saw that the notebook was open to a drawing of a chessboard with a lot of arrows and cross-outs. This surprised Ollie. In her mind, Coco Zintner and chess diagrams didn't go together.

Ollie looked closer. Coco's drawing was a picture of an endgame, the last few moves of a match. The white side was losing. Before she could stop herself, Ollie muttered, "White castle to h6 and mate in five moves."

The new girl jumped, looked at her paper, then looked up at Ollie. A sunrise of openmouthed delight dawned on her face. In fact, she looked so happy that it made Ollie feel snappish. "Obviously," she added.

Snappish because of memory. Her mother had been a math professor at Evansburg College. She had taught Ollie math with games. Multiplication, division. Later algebra, and then geometry: symbols like magic spells, written on the skin of the world. She would entertain Ollie on hikes by setting her a problem at the trailhead and asking for an answer at the top of the mountain. One night, Ollie had overheard her mom whisper to her dad, "Well, Olivia is better than I was at her age. Let's try her on music and chess; they often go with math."

They had put the upright piano in the entryway of the Egg (the only place it would fit) and Ollie had begun plinking out songs; they had given her a chess set, and Ollie still remembered the taste of triumph, the celebratory piece of apple pie, on the evening she'd first beaten her mom without having been spotted a piece.

But the piano had sat silent for nearly a year now, and Ollie's dad wasn't good at chess.

Coco took no notice of Ollie's tone. *"You play chess?"* she said, shrill with delight.

Ollie supposed Coco had a right to be surprised. Coco hadn't known Ollie *before*. Coco was so excited, she had begun to wrinkle the paper on her lap. "Want to play? I don't have a set, but we can call it—"

"No," said Ollie.

"But . . ." Coco drooped at once.

"Gotta go." Ollie beat a hasty retreat down the aisle of the bus and halted next to Brian.

"Move," she said.

Mike Campbell and Phil Greenblatt peered interestedly over the seat in front. Brian looked like he was trying extra hard to be cool. "What if I don't want to? *Ollie-pop.*"

That dumb nickname. Her ears burned. "Not my problem," Ollie retorted. "It's not my fault you're wider than you are tall."

Mike and Phil laughed. Brian, to Ollie's surprise, suddenly slid over. Was it her imagination or was he looking embarrassed too? "All yours," he said.

Ollie sat down, keeping a suspicious eye on Brian. First he got her out of detention, and now he was . . . A thought struck her. "Did you *save* me a seat?" she asked.

"What?" said Brian. He was definitely red about the ears. "No."

She eyed him. He turned studiously to look out the window.

Ollie stared, and then shrugged. Let boys be a mystery for another day; there was the mystery of her book in front of her. Ollie opened up *Small Spaces*.

"Jon," I said. "What are you going to do?"

"Go with him," said Jonathan, his voice thick with despair. "I promised. In exchange for Caleb. I have to go. Or—or he'll take Caleb instead. We made a bargain, you see. But it might not be for long." He tried to sound reassuring, but I don't think even he believed it. "Until the mist becomes rain."

"What does that mean?"

"I don't know. But—Beth, he kept his side of the

bargain. Caleb died the night I told him you and I were engaged."

I trembled. "No—no, he didn't. Jon, you're not thinking properly. Of course he didn't die. He came home. He came home three nights later."

"Yes," said Jon. "Because the smiling man and I made a bargain. I think he knew he was getting the better end of the deal and that is why he smiled. Caleb died thirty years ago, and now I have to go into the mist."

"What are you reading, Ollie?" asked Brian.

Ollie looked up. Was Brian trying to be nice *again?* People's parents did sometimes tell their kids to be nice to *that girl* because you know what happened to the *poor thing.* The thought put a nasty edge in her voice when she answered, "Are you blind? A book."

"Ah," said Brian. He angled his head to get a look at the book's cover. "What book? I've never seen it before. Did you get it from the library?"

How would you know what's in the library, Ollie thought. "It's called *Small Spaces,*" she said, biting off each word. She lifted the cover to show him. "Which you could read for yourself. If you could read." Usually one nasty remark was enough to put people off being nice.

There was a small silence. "Well, I only learned reeling and writhing," Brian said conversationally to the top of her head. "And *then* the different branches of arithmetic—ambition, distraction, uglification, and derision."

What? Ollie knew where she'd heard that sentence before. She could feel her mouth sagging open in a way that she didn't think people did in real life.

"Mystery, ancient and modern," Brian went on, leaning back in his seat, looking smug. "With seaography, then drawling—but, whoops, they forgot reading. Sorry to bug you."

And with that he leaned forward to join the conversation between Mike and Phil: "Yeah, when he took that third shot, and faked the goalie left—"

You might get to know characters in books, Ollie thought, but getting to know a human was an entirely different thing. She tried to keep reading but couldn't. Her mom's voice was lodged in her brain too deeply to be forgettable. *You were rude, Olivia,* said her mother's voice. *You judged him and he didn't deserve it.*

Ollie told herself she didn't care.

Yes she did.

She shut her book, a finger holding the page.

"It's about a girl named Beth," she said to Brian. "She lives on an old farm called Smoke Hollow. Sort of like Misty Valley." Then Ollie couldn't resist asking, "Have you memorized *Alice in Wonderland?*"

"Not really. Bits," said Brian, looking cautious. As though

he were admitting to something too weird for a hockey star. "I just liked the words in that part. I can tell you most of 'Jabberwocky' if you like, for all the good it will do you."

He stopped talking. Ollie had stopped listening. She was looking past him, out through the curtains of rain. Who was that? A little boy in a brown coat, standing just at the edge of the cornfield. But his face was still and colorless. "Who is that?" Ollie said, pointing.

Brian turned his head to follow her finger. "I don't see anything."

He looked like—no. What was she thinking? It was just a scarecrow in a suit. Ollie didn't like scarecrows. When the light was weird, like now, in the rain, they almost looked alive. Stupid scarecrows.

"Never mind," Ollie said.

They passed a sign. MISTY VALLEY FARM AND GARDENS.

In the last moments before the bus rolled to a stop, Ollie paged back to the book's epigraph.

Avoid large places at night . . .

Ollie touched the words, wishing she understood.

The sun was coming out. The rain had slowed to a drizzle. Thick, surprising sunbeams slanted through the clouds.

The bus turned in the farm gate. They parked in a big gravel parking lot and the engine cut out. A few people had put down their windows when the rain stopped. The smell of cows and garlic floated in. The students filed off the bus. When she got to the front, Ollie glanced sideways toward the bus driver. To her surprise, he was gone. A tall woman was waiting at the bus door, directing the kids as they came off. She wore a plaid shirt and muddy boots.

Ollie saw her and froze.

Linda Webster, owner of Misty Valley Farm, was the woman from yesterday, the woman whose book Ollie had stolen.

8

"WELCOME TO MISTY VALLEY!" Ms. Webster called, smiling. Her face looked pleasant now, wholesomely weathered. Her eyes were calm, sane. The streaky black makeup, the tears, the skull smile were all gone. She might have been a totally different person, except Ollie recognized her long amber-honey braid. The bus sighed and settled. People were clogging up the aisle. Ollie hurriedly ducked her head, coughed into her hand, hoping Ms. Webster hadn't gotten a good look at her. She got off the bus and hid in a group of her classmates. *Small Spaces* seemed to be lying extra heavy in her backpack.

Maybe Ms. Webster's not crazy? Maybe she's really scared of something?

But what?

Ollie looked around. A red farmhouse stood on the

top of a little rise. Just below lay a long, low barn. Behind the barn was a slim slice of pasture, muddy and gently rolling, with a herd of dairy cows. Chickens wandered around the open spaces between the buildings, pecking. Next to the cows, a field of late sunflowers nodded in the breeze. The sound of Lethe Creek came faintly to her ears, and the sun peered through the hurrying clouds, turning the leaves gold.

Really nothing to be scared of. It was beautiful. Except . . . A group of three scarecrows stood on the edge of the parking lot, smiling stitched-on smiles. Their garden-rake hands were raised to wave. The tips of the rakes gleamed in the sun.

Ollie kept turning. More scarecrows. Scarecrows everywhere. Someone had set up scarecrows between buildings, in the vegetable garden, on stakes in the cornfield. Their hands were trowels or garden rakes. Their smiles had been sewn or painted on. Scarecrows, Ollie thought uneasily, should not be used for decoration. Piles of pumpkins were much better.

But creepy though the scarecrows were, they hardly explained Linda Webster crying by the creek the day before.

"Man," said Brian Battersby's voice behind her. "I wouldn't want to meet these guys on a dark night."

Ollie turned. Brian was eyeing a particularly sinister scarecrow: tall, dressed in an old-fashioned black suit. It had garden forks for hands. "No," Ollie said, a little puzzled, but in complete agreement. *Why* was Brian even talking to her? "I wouldn't either."

Brian grinned at her and reached up to adjust the tall scarecrow's straw hat. "Good thing they're just scarecrows. Have fun today, Ollie-pop."

He sauntered away with Phil and Mike.

———

"Come over here, please! Gather round!"

The sixth grade clustered around Ms. Webster, except for Ollie, who hung back. "Welcome!" Ms. Webster said. "We have a *lovely* program for you—" Just then, the bus driver popped up beside her: pale, gray bearded, and red lipped. Where had he been? Also . . . did Ms. Webster flinch away from him slightly? Was *he* the one Ms. Webster was scared of? Maybe *he'd* made her go dump a book into Lethe Creek? But why?

The bus driver's skin really was the gray-white of an old mushroom.

Ollie loved mushrooms. On weekends, she and her mom used to go foraging for wild ones. It had been an autumn day like this one, clouds chasing sun, when they had found Ollie's first chicken-of-the-woods. "These are pretty rare, Olivia," her mom had said, glowing. "Look. Chicken-of-the-woods only grow out of the hearts of dying trees." She tapped the elm in question. "This tree is a goner. Forest rangers don't like to see chicken-of-the-woods because they mean the good hardwoods are dying. But this mushroom . . ."

"What?" Ollie cried, stroking the orange-red thing with a forefinger.

"You'll see," said her mom, smiling, pulling out her pocketknife.

Sure enough, the second they got home, her dad whooped and said, "I'll make the batter. No, sit down, both of you; you'll just get oil everywhere."

That night, they feasted on chicken-fried wild mushroom with mashed potatoes. Afterward, Ollie and her mom swam in the freezing creek and ate homemade ice cream. It was the best of days. But when Ollie's mom came to tuck her in that night, she found Ollie crying.

"Olivia, are you okay?" she asked. "Does your tummy hurt?"

Ollie shook her head. "I'm sad for the tree—the tree where the mushroom came from. It doesn't seem fair that it gave us the best and yummiest mushroom and now it's just going to *die*." She buried her face in her pillow. That was back when she could cry over dumb things like elm trees.

Her mother sighed and said, "No, it's not fair. But the tree gave us a gift. Even bad things can lead to good. Maybe in sad times, it helps to think of that."

"Maybe," said Ollie, unconvinced.

"If you like," said her mom, giving her a hug, "we can go visit the tree tomorrow and say thank you."

"I'd like that," said Ollie, and wiped her nose.

But they never did. First it rained and then it snowed, and then Ollie got older and forgot. Now they wouldn't ever and it didn't matter. Why did she even have to think of it?

9

"*MISTY VALLEY MAKES* most of its money from eco-tourism," Dad had told Ollie on the way to school. "That means Linda Webster isn't selling her milk for big bucks. She's getting the big bucks from idiots who want to milk the cow. And I mean actual big bucks. She just bought a Mercedes for going down to Boston—this town's never seen an ordinary farmer do so well."

Most milking barns had machinery to do the milking. Linda Webster's cows were led in on halters and milked into buckets. Ms. Webster even had one cow who was on a weird milking schedule so she could be milked for tour groups, not at 5:00 a.m.

This cow was tied in one of the milking stalls when the sixth grade clomped in. A man was sitting on a stool next to her, stroking her udder, humming under his breath. He had a shock of pale hair, even lighter than Coco's, curling over his forehead. His face was angular. There was a dimple on one side of his mouth.

Up ahead, Lily Mayhew was walking with Jenna Gehrmann. They both were struck with a severe case of giggles.

"This is Seth," said Ms. Webster. Seth's eyes were dark and just a little green, like looking into a pond on a cloudy day. "He helps out around the farm," Ms. Webster said. "Can anyone tell me what he's doing now?"

"Getting her to let the milk down," said Mike Campbell. He was one of the farm kids. *Obviously* was in his voice. A third of the class lived on dairy farms.

"This is Cora," said Seth. He had a soft, pleasant voice, but it cut through the farm kids' impatience, the hockey bros' chatter, even Lily Mayhew's giggling. They all quieted down. Seth, Ollie thought, would not stand for nonsense from kids or cows. Probably Cora didn't dare kick the milk bucket. Seth started to milk her in steady strokes.

The bus driver was still a step behind Ms. Webster. But if she was scared of him now, she showed no sign of it. "Cora is a *Jersey* cow," Ms. Webster said. She went into detail about the nature of Jersey cows. Ollie's attention wandered.

A black cat was watching the milking. He was big and sleek: the kind of cat that tortures mice and steals cream. Without looking around, Seth lifted the cow's teat and aimed at the cat, who caught the milk in its mouth with a practiced air. A few kids applauded. The cat twined itself around Seth's legs, purring. Cora shivered and stamped. Seth jerked his chin. The cat left. *The one cow in Vermont that's afraid of barn cats, and the one cat in the world that obeys orders,* Ollie thought. But still, nothing she'd seen explained Ms. Webster's tears the day before.

Mike, Phil, and Brian were passing Mike's phone around, grinning. Mr. Easton reached over Brian's head and confiscated it. The class snickered. Mike looked wounded.

"Cora is our oldest," Ms. Webster said, an edge in her voice. Well, the sixth grade wasn't exactly hanging on her every word. "She doesn't give much milk anymore. But she is gentle." Cora chewed her cud and blinked at them. "Perfect to meet guests. Would anyone like to milk her?"

Seth stood up, leaving the bucket down by Cora's feet.

Even the kids who lived on dairy farms rarely milked cows by hand. Cows were used to getting milked by machines and didn't like people. No one wanted to get kicked by an angry cow. The whole sixth grade hung back. Lily and Jenna giggled and pushed each other forward, but neither volunteered.

"Someone volunteer or I'm picking someone," said Mr. Easton.

"I want to be first!" squeaked Coco Zintner suddenly. "Let me go!" She pushed forward. "Hello," she said delightedly to the cow, and reached up to give Cora a pat. Some of the farm kids snorted. Coco's parents had only moved the family up north that year, to "get back to nature." Things that bored the local kids—like cows—all delighted Coco.

"Get back to nature," Ollie had once overheard Ms. Mouton whisper to Mr. Easton, sighing. "I wonder if nature will survive it."

Coco stepped toward the milking stool. "Wait now, easy . . ." began Mr. Easton.

Too late. Coco tripped on the milk bucket and went flying. Cora, startled, jumped and shuffled. The whole class laughed. Even Ms. Webster cracked a smile. Well, Coco *had* looked ridiculous, going splat on the barn floor.

Only Seth didn't laugh. He looked thoughtful. Coco burst into tears. The noise was unbearable: Coco crying and kids laughing. Ollie decided that she'd had enough. She edged toward the barn door, then slipped out. Mr. Easton didn't see her. He was preoccupied with Coco, who had a bloody chin. If anyone asked, Ollie decided, she would just say she'd gone to the bathroom and gotten lost.

———

Outside it was cool and windy. Ollie took a deep breath of *not* cow-smelling air. There was a vegetable garden behind the house full of runner beans and kale, turnips and carrots. She went inside.

A garden after rain was much better than that echoing

barn. Ollie loved gardens. Her mom always planted a garden in the summer; Ollie had been snacking from vegetable patches since she was old enough to chew. Ollie broke a broccoli flower out of its stalk and ate it happily.

Munching, she wandered toward the middle of the garden. Three scarecrows stood in the very center, holding hands. They smiled big smiles at each other, their lips pierced with thread. The biggest scarecrow wore overalls. His smile was more like a snarl. A crow perched on his head. *Kraak,* said the crow, beating its wings.

"A great job you're doing," Ollie told the scarecrows. She bent for a rock, aimed just below the crow. She'd once made the mistake of aiming *at* a bird and never forgot how terrible she'd felt when she knocked it out of the air.

She caught the scarecrow in the forehead. The crow flew up, unhurt, cawing indignantly, as the scarecrow's head burst open.

Ollie got a good look at what her rock had left—ripped-open burlap, leaking straw, and, below it, the big yarn grin, unchanged. She shuddered and hurried away.

To her left she could see where the berry bushes grew in summer. To her right was the edge of the forest, and the faint silver gleam of the creek.

Ollie stepped into the forest. It was like a different world there, golden with autumn. Wet earth squished underfoot. It would be a good morning for mushrooms.

Footsteps crunched in the leaves. "Hello?" Ollie called.

Silence. Maybe she'd just heard a chipmunk. She went a little farther in. A stick cracked right next to her. She jumped and turned. No chipmunk. No one. But she caught sight of a small iron gate. Ollie went closer. The gate led to an old cemetery with graves tilted like bad teeth.

Ollie put a hand on the gate. The hinges gave with a shrill *wheeee*. Ollie looked around to see if anyone had heard. No one had, of course. She was definitely alone.

She tried to ignore the shivery feeling going up her spine.

She slipped inside the cemetery. Green gravestones stood in messy rows with their inscriptions blurred by time. Ollie brushed dirt off the first. *Ezekiel Hopkins*, the first one read, *b. 1836, d. 1869 of the falling of a tree.*

Sorry, Ezekiel, Ollie thought.

She went on to the next. *Fanny Collar*, she read. *Nov. 11, 1801—June 28, 1886, wife of Amasa Piper, first white child born near this spot, God Have Mercy on Your Servant.*

That's a weird thing to be remembered for, thought Ollie.

A big stone, with a plaque and a long list of names. *Dust to dust*, it said. *But they will rise up out of the ashes.*

The schoolhouse fire, Ollie thought. *There is a memorial, after all.*

Then she spotted three headstones a little apart from the others, right against the tumbledown fence at the back. These three were in a cluster, one big and two smaller. They lay at awkward angles, as though someone had not taken care where they put them. Ollie, curious, went closer.

Jonathan Webster, Elizabeth Webster, said the bigger one, *d. 1894. May the dead lie quiet.* Ollie frowned.

Caleb Webster, said the headstone on the left.

Catherine Webster, said the headstone on the right.

Ollie's fingertips got cold.

"Four graves, three stones," said a raspy voice. "But only two sets of bones."

Ollie squeaked, jumped, and whirled. The bus driver stood behind her. Where had he come from? The ground was thick with dead leaves—they should have rustled. Alone in the woods, the bus driver's, red lips, his mushroom-gray skin, and his sideways grin weren't just strange—they scared her.

"Yeah," said Ollie, heart beating fast. "Sorry, I got lost, was just heading back . . ."

She trailed off. The bus driver did not react.

Ollie's heart beat faster and faster.

The driver began to whisper, and it took Ollie a moment to realize he was murmuring in a singsong:

> *On a fair and sunny day*
> *Two grown boys went out to play*
> *All day they ran and ran*
> *But only one went home—*

Ollie stepped back again. Another step and she'd be leaning on Cathy Webster's tilted grave. "But—"

Jon, my dear, said their kind mother
Where on earth is your little brother?
Don't know? Oh, foolish child
Enough nonsense, you are exiled
Till you bring him home for supper.

Ollie didn't know what to say. The three gravestones loomed in her imagination big as barns at her back. "I like poems," she said a little at random, talking to keep herself from being frightened. "I memorized one from a book I liked, *The Grey King*. 'On the day of the dead'—"

"No," said the bus driver.

Something cold and flat in his voice silenced Ollie. Her heart was going rabbit fast now, with the iron fence of the graveyard behind her and the bus driver in front. "Listen, girl," said the driver. "*Listen*. There's no time. Four graves, three stones, two sets of bones. But all four souls unquiet. The mist comes off the creek when the year's turning and—"

"What on *earth*?" said a new voice.

The bus driver went still, except that his tongue shot round, just once, and licked his red lips. Seth, the pale-haired farmhand, was standing at the gate of the grave-yard. "Is he scaring you?" he asked Ollie. He had his hands

81

in his pockets. He didn't raise his voice. But the bus driver was backing up.

"Never mind, never mind," said the driver, his voice almost a whine. "Just telling this little inquisitive one some history. Nothing wrong with history."

Seth raised a pale brow. "Nothing at all wrong with history. The bigger problem is cornering a kid in a graveyard."

Seth's voice was completely ordinary, comforting. Ollie felt the little scared knot inside her begin to ease. "Go on," said Seth to the driver. "I'll walk her back."

Without another word, the bus driver hunched his shoulders and hurried out the gate and up the road.

"Got tired of Cora, did you?" Seth asked her.

Still breathless with fright, Ollie managed, "It was noisy in there."

"Well, you'll have that," said Seth. "Kids and all." He waved Ollie out of the graveyard and shut the gate behind them. Ollie, looking at the back of his head, wondered why she was stuck with brown hair when some people got unlikely shades of blond.

"Is it true?" Ollie asked as they walked.

Seth turned to her with a face politely questioning.

"What the bus driver said. Are there only two bodies buried in those three graves?" She pointed to the three at the back of the graveyard.

Seth's glance sharpened. "He said that? I'm going to

really have to make sure that guy stops lurking around. Use your head. How would he know who's buried down there? It's not like we're running around digging up hundred-year-old graves. Just for the sake of ghost stories."

"So there is a ghost story?"

When Seth smiled, it softened the angular bones of his face. Ollie found herself warming to him. "Come on, kid," said Seth. "There's always a ghost story. Look around. How long have people lived on this land? There's us, yeah, but before us, there were those people in that graveyard back there. Fanny Collar—you saw her, right?—on her grave it says that she married the first white child born in Evansburg—why do you think that was even a thing? Because before them, there were the Abenaki, and *they* had this land and farmed it and died on it and wrote their own ghost stories while people died of plague in the streets of London." Seth's eyes were far away. "So yes, there is *always* a ghost story. Put that in your pipe and smoke it. Wherever you go in this big, gorgeous, hideous world, there is a ghost story waiting for you. Maybe made-up or maybe not, but that's no excuse for that guy to lurk around graveyards and scare kids."

They were getting to the edge of the wood. Ollie could see the scarecrows peeking over the carrot tops in the vegetable garden. "You should probably stay out of graveyards this close to Halloween," said Seth. "I think the others are in the horse barn." He gave her a push in the right direction and started off toward the cornfield, whistling.

So much for sneaking off. She couldn't very well say she'd gotten lost now. Ollie headed toward the horse barn. In the normal light of the barnyard, Ollie was less sure that something weird was going on. Ms. Webster probably had a well-hidden mental illness that made her panic and throw books into rivers. Or maybe she just hated books. The author of *Small Spaces* had probably visited the farm once. She had seen the graves, heard the story, gotten inspired. That was the only logical explanation.

The bus driver was standing at the edge of the vegetable garden. She had to walk past him. Ollie lifted her chin and stiffened her spine. *Linda Webster is maybe crazy and this guy certainly is, but Seth is nice, the sun is shining . . .*

"They're still waiting, you know," whispered the driver as Ollie went by. "Beth and Cathy. You can hear them crying at night, or calling the boys. But they don't answer."

Ollie gave up all pretense of coolness and ran toward the horse barn.

10

BY THE TIME Ollie caught up, the sixth grade was trekking toward a patch of sunflowers whose petals had withered, their pods rattling with seeds. Ollie tried to sneak in with the group, but Mr. Easton spotted her. "Ollie!" he called.

She altered course. Mr. Easton was frowning. "I didn't see you in the milk shed. I didn't spot you in the horse barn either. Did you go outside?"

Ollie debated lying, decided Mr. Easton would know it, and said, "Yes."

Mr. Easton looked concerned. "Did you need some quiet time?"

Ollie suddenly wanted to yell. Quiet time, always quiet time, as if she could make her own head and heart be quiet.

"Yes," said Ollie again.

Mr. Easton sighed. "I understand. But next time, tell

me. Don't just sneak off. Now we're going to harvest some sunflower seeds and then it'll be time for lunch."

Mr. Easton, Ollie thought, was nice.

Lunch was delicious. Misty Valley had an outdoor bread oven, which Seth handled with an old-fashioned bread paddle, a streak of flour on one sharp cheekbone. Lily Mayhew went back three times for bread, giggling. She and Jenna egged each other on. Even Ollie went back once, and when Seth winked at her, she smiled at him. He hadn't winked at Lily Mayhew.

The bread was good. It had a thick golden crust and pale insides. There was honey you could put on top and a salty sort of butter. With the bread went a red tomato soup. "The last of the fresh tomatoes!" proclaimed Ms. Webster, presiding over the pot and big rounds of farmhouse cheese.

Waiting in the soup line, Ollie decided that she was fed up with being puzzled. When she raised her bowl to have it filled with tomato soup, she met Ms. Webster's eyes.

"Hi," she said, holding out her bowl.

The lady in front of her suddenly wore such a cold, sinking expression of fright that Ollie felt a prickling of nervousness between her own shoulder blades. "So nice to see you again," said Ollie, in her best innocent voice.

Ms. Webster slopped soup toward Ollie's bowl, but her trembling hand missed and sent cream of tomato all over the ground. "Clumsy of me. Um—no," Ms. Webster stammered. "No—no, I don't think so. I mean, I don't remember meeting you. Sorry." She ladled Ollie more soup with hands that still trembled.

"I'm reading it," said Ollie, abandoning pretense. "I'll give it back to you if you want. But I just have some questions."

Ms. Webster's pumpkin-head grin was more fake than ever. "Oh—I can't imagine what you mean. Go along, dear." She turned sharply to serve soup to the next kid, putting her back to Ollie.

Frowning, Ollie got bread and cheese and pumpkin pie and went to a table. She was more confused than ever. She wished she could sneak off by herself and finish *Small Spaces*, but Mr. Easton was keeping a close eye on her.

When they finished serving food, Seth and Ms. Webster and the bus driver sat down with Mr. Easton. Ollie watched them closely. Ms. Webster was talking with frantic animation, like she was an actor in a play. Seth didn't say much although sometimes he smiled. The bus driver was hunched over his food, eating as though he were starving, off a plate piled high. The food disappeared in a blink. His red mouth bit, gulped, swallowed.

It had to be him that Ms. Webster was scared of. Why? What connection did *he* have to a book called *Small Spaces*? Why would he want Ms. Webster to get rid of it?

Coco Zintner plopped down on the bench opposite Ollie, breaking her chain of thought. Coco had a *Cars* Band-Aid on her chin, and her eyes were red.

"I hate them," said Coco. "They all laughed at me. No one helped."

Ollie hadn't helped either. "Sorry," she mumbled, still keeping an eye on the adults.

"You helped me yesterday," said Coco. "I never said thanks. So, thanks."

Ollie didn't say anything.

"Don't *you* hate them?" said Coco, with a sweep of her arm to indicate their class. Ollie hurriedly rescued her cup of water, which Coco had almost sent into her lap. "You always sit by yourself."

Ollie thought about explaining, and then she just said, "No. I don't hate anyone." That was true. She just didn't care enough to try to be friends anymore. She hadn't cared about much of anything in almost a year. She looked down again, finding her place on the page.

"Then why do you sit by yourself?" asked Coco.

Ollie said nothing.

"Is it because your mom died?" Coco pressed.

Ollie looked up, stomach churning. She didn't hate her classmates for the most part, but she *did* hate Coco just then. Pretty Coco with her pink hair and her stupid crying eyes and her mom at home.

"None of your business!" Ollie snapped. "Or don't you have any brain at all in your stupid pink head?"

A murmur of appalled delight ran through the sixth grade. Coco stared at Ollie, her mouth open, her eyes filling with tears once again.

Ollie got up and ran, book in her pocket, backpack over her shoulder, leaving the rest of her bread uneaten.

11

THE LAST THING before the sixth grade went home was to stand in line to have their picture taken in the middle of a group of three scarecrows. Ollie lined up with everyone else, but she was almost bouncing with impatience. She wanted so badly to read, it felt like her book was burning a hole in her backpack. Mr. Easton looked happy. The sun was vivid now; the clouds had all burned away. They had spent the whole day at the farm, and, except for Coco's chin, the trip had gone pretty well.

The bus driver was still hanging around. He eyed the sixth grade as though he were picking out which chicken to chop for dinner, Ollie thought.

Mr. Easton tried to make small talk. "A lot of scarecrows you've got here," he said. "Where'd you find the time to make so many?"

Ollie hadn't thought of that. She wondered if there

were other farmworkers they hadn't seen. How many people did it take to run a farm?

"They were already here," said the bus driver.

"The scarecrows?" said Mr. Easton. "Where'd they come from?"

"Here," said the bus driver again. "All here." Now he was looking over Mr. Easton's shoulder *straight* at Ollie. She wanted to slink away. "Eyes open, just ready to be stood up."

Mr. Easton looked interested. "They are in such good condition," he said. "I wonder how old they are."

The bus driver just shrugged and smiled. He was still looking at Ollie. "Old enough," he said. "Old enough."

———

The clouds were filling in as the sun slanted west. Twilight had arrived by the time the sixth grade piled into the steamy bus. There was much less noise than that morning. Lunch and horses, milking cows and photos had worn them out.

"It was good to meet you, Olivia," Seth said.

"You too," said Ollie. She didn't even correct him when he called her Olivia. She thought of telling him everything, asking him if he knew what Ms. Webster was afraid of. "Mr. Seth—" she began.

But Mr. Easton broke in. "On the bus!" he called. "Hurry up! Got to get to school by pickup time."

Ollie hesitated, torn, and then Seth had already turned toward the main barn, whistling again. He gave Ollie a last, thoughtful glance over his shoulder.

Ollie climbed onto the bus.

Ms. Webster watched them go from the gravel driveway. As the sun hid behind clouds, the cheery expression seemed to leach out of her face, leaving it gray and old, exhausted. She looked just like she had crying by the creek, except this time her eyes were dry, her face hard. The black cat ("His name's Behemoth," Seth had told her when Ollie asked, making her laugh) sat behind Ms. Webster. His tail was curled neatly about his feet, his eyes bright in the gathering dusk.

Ollie sank down in her seat, ready to get home to the Egg. Hopefully Dad was making something yummy. Lasagna, or his famous cornbread-mole-squash potpie. Ollie, to make up for yesterday, would eat every bite. Then she would finish *Small Spaces* downstairs by the woodstove with a mug of hot chocolate. Once she finished, she would tell her dad about the farm mystery. He would be intrigued. They would pass theories back and forth. She would even laugh at his jokes.

Coco Zintner kept trying to apologize. Ollie ignored her. Coco tried one last time on the bus. "Hey, Ollie," she said. "Ollie, I—"

Ollie, tired and at the end of her temper, was about to

say something she would have regretted, but Mr. Easton saved her. "Come on!" he called. "Get in your seats, all of you! We're moving out!"

Coco sat down, looking unhappy. The engine roared; the bus started off.

Ollie took the seat next to Brian again. She wondered what Brian, who quoted *Alice's Adventures in Wonderland*, would think about the mystery of Misty Valley and *Small Spaces*.

She didn't know what to think of it herself. She opened her book.

> *Three nights later, Jonathan disappeared.*
>
> *He had made a will. The farm was mine, for my lifetime, and our children's after I was gone. The farm I now leave to you, Margaret, my dearest daughter.*
>
> *He also left me a letter. "Do not try to find me," he wrote. "I love you. I am sorry."*
>
> *But we searched. Of course we searched. We found nothing.*
>
> *A week after his brother's disappearance, Caleb came to me. "I know where Jon is," he said.*
>
> *"I know what you're thinking," I said. "But the smiling man isn't real. Jon just made him up. He was frightened and he felt guilty and made him up." But even as I said it, I didn't believe it, and Caleb knew I didn't.*

"The smiling man pulled me out of the river," said Caleb. "I can't remember anything else from that night. But I remember his hands on mine, and mine were blue." Caleb paused. "Jonathan's not gone, you know. At night, I can hear his footsteps." Caleb swallowed. "I can go to him. I can go to where he is. So Jon won't be alone."

I shouldn't have said it. My dear Margaret, I shouldn't have. But I did. "Go to him, then, madman," I spat. "If you think you can. Don't come back. It is your fault he is gone."

Caleb wasn't angry. He stood silent a moment. Then he bent and whispered in my ear, "Until the mist becomes rain."

Then he was gone.

I never saw Caleb or Jonathan again.

Something changed in the quality of the noise on the bus. Ollie looked up from her book, frowning. The shouting had dropped, and even the monotonous urging from Mr. Easton to *sit down, please, and be quiet* seemed different—distracted, puzzled.

Ollie looked out the window, peering around Brian.

A heavy fog had descended on the road, the black tops of trees poking up like drowning fingers. The left side of the road was forest. On the right, the cornfields stretched out, guarded by scowling scarecrows. The mist was so dense that it threw the headlights back into their eyes. The bus was rolling along at a crawl. Ollie's hands tightened involuntarily on her book.

There were mutters all around, nervous giggling.

"So weird."

"Look at that fog."

"I have to pee."

The bus was crawling slower and slower. The mist thickened. Ollie didn't recognize where they were; she didn't even know how long they'd been driving. She stared out the window. *When the mist rises . . .*

But the year wasn't turning. Also, her book was just a story.

They drifted to a halt. The bus coughed and died.

For a moment, total silence.

Then a burst of noise.

"I think the bus broke down!"

"I want to go home!"

"We're lost!" yelled Mike Campbell, even though that was stupid. How could they be lost?

Ollie was still staring out the window. The yellow autumn trees had turned black and spindly, as though winter had come in the last three minutes. The broad, smooth country road had become an old, cracked ribbon, running away and vanishing into the trees, still lapped in mist.

Where were they?

Slowly, the bus driver stood up. The shouting died away. The driver turned around. He seemed to have gotten both taller and wider. "Well," said the driver, surveying them, "best get moving. At nightfall they'll come for the rest of you."

Then he smiled, tongue flicking red against his teeth.

12

THE BUS FILLED with laughter. Mr. Easton chuckled and pulled out his phone. "Good joke," he said. "Bus broken down? I'll just notify the farm—and the school—we'll have to get a replacement out, if we can't fix it. We might be here awhile. Well, no day is perfect."

Ollie, frowning, got out her own phone.

Somewhere over her head, she could feel Brian eyeing it. "I didn't know they still made those." Ollie's phone was a heavy thing that flipped open. She had to text by scrolling through numeric options, and it took forever. But the phone had been her mother's. Dad had tried to get her a new one for her birthday, but she had screamed at him and thrown it across the room.

NO SERVICE, said the screen.

"My phone doesn't work," said the whole bus in complaining chorus.

Ollie looked out the window again. How long had they been driving? She had gotten muddled while reading. The farm was not *that* far away—and they definitely had service there. She couldn't think of any no-service spots between the school and the farm, but that didn't mean there weren't any.

The noise in the bus was rising: a discontented, phoneless howl.

"Enough!" bellowed Mr. Easton. He had already stowed his own phone. "Well, bad luck," he said to the driver. "Care to pop the hood? I'll hop out and see what the trouble is."

The driver pulled the lever for the hood. But he didn't get out to help Mr. Easton. He sank back down in his seat and stared straight ahead. Mr. Easton shrugged, pulled the lever for the door himself, and went outside.

A creepy feeling ran down Ollie's spine. What had the driver said? *They'll come for the rest of you.* Mr. Easton thought it was a joke; Ollie remembered the driver whispering in the graveyard and she wasn't so sure.

The inside of her window was fogging up. Ollie reached over Brian, wiped the sleeve of her sweater on the glass, and looked. The trees were bare. The road stretched away flat before and behind them. The grass between the road and the forest was long and wet and flopped onto the asphalt.

How long until dark?

The overhead lights flickered. Ollie felt a cold tug

of memory. Hadn't Beth said something about candles flickering?

But this was totally different, she reassured herself. The bus had broken down, that was why the lights were blinking. What time was it? There were only dashes on Ollie's phone where the time should have been.

Ollie's watch was also a compass and an altimeter. It had been her mother's. Ollie glanced at it, but only out of reflex. Ollie's mom had worn it that last day, and it didn't work anymore. The watch gave wildly varying altitudes and completely inaccurate times; the compass did not point north. Now there was a countdown where the time should have been (45:02), and just below that, the digital readout said RUN in gray letters, flickering like the lights.

The word gave Ollie a strange, sharp jolt. She looked back toward the front of the bus. Mr. Easton was still outside. The driver hadn't moved. Maybe the bus would be moving in a minute.

Or maybe it wouldn't. Ollie grabbed her backpack, so that Phil couldn't put a frog or something in it, and marched up the aisle. All around, her classmates talked, laughed, yelled. She ignored them. Deliberately she took a step across the yellow line in the front of the bus. You weren't supposed to cross that line, but the bus driver didn't even turn his head.

"What happens at nightfall?" Ollie demanded, wishing her voice didn't sound so breathless.

The bus driver's mouth curved up at a strange angle, as though a child had drawn the smile on. His tongue and his gums were very red. He said nothing.

"Who is coming for us?" Ollie asked, getting control of her voice.

Still no answer.

Ollie clamped down on her fear. After all, Mr. Easton was right outside and the bus was full of people. From the front of the bus came a series of loud bangs and some un-teacher-like swearing.

Suddenly, the bus driver said, "Can't tell you. Already said too much."

Won't tell me, Ollie thought. *Not can't.* She remembered lunchtime, the driver's vast plate of food, his red, biting mouth. Maybe . . . "Are you hungry?"

This time the driver turned to face her. Ollie got a terrible shock. His eyes had turned white, white as an egg, pupil-less. He might have been blind except he was definitely looking at her. His teeth were perfectly white too, sharp against red lips.

Ollie reached into her lunch box, got out a quarter of her turkey sandwich. The driver licked his lips and reached out one stealthy, grabby hand.

Ollie stepped back. "No," she said. "It's mine." Heroines

in books always sounded brave, but to her own ears, Ollie sounded scared. "I'll trade you for it."

The white eyes narrowed.

"You answer my questions," Ollie said. "I'll give you my sandwich."

A long silence. "Shouldn't," grunted the driver.

"Fine, then," said Ollie. "See if I care." And she lifted her sandwich as though she meant to take a huge bite, even though she wasn't hungry, not at all.

Right before she sank her teeth into it, the driver asked, "What questions, little girl?"

The noise at the back of the bus was deafening. Probably no one could hear this conversation but them. Ollie thought hard, keeping an eye on his thick fingers.

"Who is coming?" she asked. "At nightfall."

The white eyes swept her up and down. Then he said, "His people. His servants."

Ollie swallowed. "Who is *he*?"

"He has many names. As many names as people have words."

That wasn't helpful. Ollie thought again. "What are his *people* going to do?"

"Take you to him. Bargain complete."

Ollie felt another twist of fear in her stomach. Trying to keep her voice steady, she said, "You said we had to get moving. Where?"

The driver smiled a little. "Forest. Get into the forest. The farther you go, the longer you stay free. Maybe you even find a way out again. Maybe."

"*Free?*" squeaked Ollie. "Who are his servants? What do they look like?"

The driver only licked his lips. "You've already asked too many questions. That was all the questions, I can't answer any more questions." His eyes skipped to the windows, to the kids in the back of the bus, and back to Ollie. "You run fast, run far, and maybe you'll get out in the end. A few do." He looked again at her classmates in the back. "They are lost already," he said, with a jerk of his chin. "They just don't know it."

"Lost? They're not lost. They're on this bus," Ollie snapped. She was getting scareder and scareder.

The driver only shrugged. "Give me food, little girl; I answered your questions." His thick fingers reached out, fluttering like spider legs.

Ollie's fingers were tingling with a slow dread. Numbly, she handed over the sandwich. Was he lying? Why would he lie?

But—arrange for the bus to break down just for a joke? That seemed ridiculous. And those white-marble eyes . . . and the book, and Ms. Webster's real terror . . . *Think, Ollie. Think.*

The quarter-sandwich disappeared in a single gulp, the way he'd inhaled his soup on the farm. "Where in the forest?" Ollie asked, low. "Please—will you tell me? Where can we go that's safe?"

Two gleams of light shone in the driver's white eyes and his lips looked moist and satisfied. "Good food," he said. "Dead meat, cold, but good. I said too much already. Besides, nowhere's safe. Not here. Not on this side of the mist."

But his eyes flicked once to the left, out into the dripping skeleton forest. Ollie followed his glance. There was a little gap in the fog, on the driver's side of the road. Between the trees was the beginning of a path. "They can move in the daytime," said the bus driver, almost too low for her to hear. "Just not while anyone's looking. They have to stand in the sunshine world too, see, to keep the door open, and that makes them weaker. More rules in the sunshine world, after all. But on this side of the mist—at night—there's only his rules. They'll grab you if they can. Now go away."

Mr. Easton came bustling in through the door of the bus.

"Ollie," he said. "What are you doing up here? Go back to your seat; there's no need to worry."

"But he said—" Ollie began, and stopped. The bus driver was sitting behind the wheel, looking straight ahead. Now he seemed perfectly—normal.

"Thanks for the snack," he said. He crumpled up the wax paper, dipped his head to lick his fingers, and seemed to peer slyly at her beneath his eyelids.

"That was nice of you, Ollie," said Mr. Easton, looking

surprised. "To think of the driver. But better to go back to your seat now. Off you go."

"But he—" Ollie stopped again. Mr. Easton looked just as he always had: cheerful, red-faced. Suddenly it seemed ridiculous to imagine monsters in the forest, to imagine that her book was anything but a story. The bus driver was joking. Her imagination had gotten away from her, just like her dad always said.

Ollie went back to her seat.

Mr. Easton was talking with the bus driver, although Ollie couldn't hear what they were saying. Finally, Mr. Easton said to the sixth grade, looking irritable, "Well, phones don't work, and I'm not having any luck with the bus. I'm going to just nip back up the road to the farm and call for help from there. Mr. Jones here"—Mr. Easton gave the driver an annoyed look—"has a bum ankle. I'll have to make the walk. Shouldn't be more than twenty minutes. You all mind the driver and I'll be back before you know it. Anyone who tries anything at *all* while I'm gone will be in detention until Christmas."

He popped out the door. Ollie wanted to warn him. But warn him of what? She didn't say anything. The thud of Mr. Easton's footsteps went the length of the bus, following the way they had come.

Then the sound was lost in the fog.

Just like that, they were alone.

A hush fell on the bus. Ollie peered out the window, but couldn't see Mr. Easton. It was as though he'd been swallowed. The mist was creeping closer.

Mike and Phil began busily sticking Coco Zintner's long hair to the back of her seat with a wad of chewing gum. The lights flickered again. Ollie's watch chimed once, softly, against her wrist. She glanced down: 39:22, said the countdown now. RUN, said the compass display, flickering.

Ollie's mouth was dry. Go out into the gray evening, into the misty forest? RUN still flickered beneath the cracked screen. Overhead the lights wavered.

The driver sat perfectly still.

Coco began to move her head in confusion. Mike and Phil sat back, looking innocent. Coco's furious scream shot through the bus. Exclamations and laughter erupted as Coco yanked her hair up from the seat back, trailing sticky strings of gum.

Coco began to cry.

I could warn everyone, Ollie thought. *But warn them about what?* She was shaking with nerves and indecision. She looked out the window again. Straight ahead was the road. To the right was the forest. Out the left-hand window was a vast, whispering cornfield.

Ollie's stomach jumped. The field was full of scare-crows. Were there—*more* of them? No, impossible.

Not impossible, Ollie thought shakily. *Very improbable.*

Ollie checked her phone one more time. NO SERVICE. *Well,* she thought determinedly, *I don't want to stay on this stupid bus anyway.* Ollie put on her rain jacket and her hat. She hoisted her polka-dot backpack higher on her shoulders.

"What are you doing, Ollie?" asked Brian. Coco was still crying. People were shouting questions at the bus driver, but he just sat there, unmoving, two hands on the wheel. The day's sun was only a memory.

Ollie said, "The driver said best get moving. I'm moving."

"*What?*" said Brian. "Where? Mr. Easton said—"

But Ollie wasn't listening. She stood up, went to the front of the bus, and looked back at her classmates. In a little place like Ben Withers, everyone knew everyone else. You went to school with the same people since kindergarten. Ollie was pretty sure no one was going to believe her. She barely believed it herself. But—what if it was true? All of it? The mist and the twilight, the bus driver's warning.

"Mr. Easton is gone," said Ollie, facing everyone down the bus aisle. She didn't think she could shout over all the noise, so she didn't try. But the people in the back shushed each other anyway. "I don't—I think maybe he's not coming back."

A startled pause, and then they laughed at her, or just rolled their eyes, or looked concerned. *Poor Ollie; you know she cracked last year.* "Come on," said a blurry chorus of voices. "He just went to the farm. He'll be back soon. He's not gone. He can't be gone."

"Gone!" Ollie snapped.

The word seemed to fall like a rock, right into all the noise. Everyone heard it, and a small, awkward stillness spread through the bus. "He went into the mist," she added. "Now it's almost dark." She could see her own breath now, Ollie realized. The bus was getting cold. The engine was turned off. The heater wasn't running. "Did you hear the driver?" she asked. *"Best get moving,* he said."

Another murmur ran through the bus. "Get moving?"

"What is she saying?"

"But Mr. Easton said he'd be right back!"

"Oh, it's just Ollie. You know she—"

"Our phones don't work," Ollie said, her voice getting stronger. "I don't think Mr. Easton is coming back. And I don't think whoever comes will want to help."

A few people were smiling, as though she'd made a good joke. Others looked concerned. The bus driver gave Ollie a sly grin. *Nice try.* Brian Battersby sat with his arms crossed, a frown on his face.

"Okay," said Ollie. "I said it. I think you should listen. I'm going to try and get away now."

She put her foot on the first step.

"Little girl," said the bus driver.

She turned around, looked into eyes like two eggs, felt

a fresh jolt of fear. "Avoid large places at night," he said. "Keep to small."

"*What does that mean?*" Ollie demanded.

The driver looked all around and then whispered, so that she could barely hear, "They are strong at night, remember? They have clever, grabbing hands, but stiff, and they can't grab you if they can't reach you. *At night!*"

"Who are they?" Ollie whispered, but the driver didn't answer. He only reached out, and pulled the lever that opened the doors. It was getting darker. The trees dripped, although it wasn't exactly raining. More of a thick, sticky mist, like being inside a cloud.

Ollie had been inside a cloud once. Her mother had taken her paragliding. Her mother loved flying. Any kind of flying.

Her father had said, *No, Ollie is too little,* but her mother had only said, *Don't worry, Rog,* and taken Ollie anyway. Ollie's mom wasn't scared of anything.

But maybe she'd been scared on that last flight, in the little single-engine. Ollie dreamed of the crash, even though she hadn't seen it. She hadn't seen the fire afterward, or the bits of broken plane stuck in a tree, the things that haunted her nightmares. She only overheard her relatives talking about it. Her father had brought the cracked watch to her at school, holding it tight in his sweaty fist. He'd sat her down right there on the bench next to the hickory tree.

Ollie had heard him out, not saying anything. Heard him out until she couldn't bear to listen anymore, and then she yelled and grabbed the watch and ran, ran for her bike, pedaled to their house, never mind the freezing rain. She had run upstairs soaking wet, shivering, to hide in her window seat. She hadn't cried. She couldn't bear to cry. Crying meant it was all real, and she didn't want it to be real.

Instead she opened a book at random, read until her eyes went blurry, and then read some more. She hadn't stopped for days. She hardly ate; she didn't sleep at all. Her dad would come up, red-eyed from crying himself, tap on her door, leave her food, go away again. She wouldn't talk to him. She barely saw him. He brought her pies, cakes, all of her favorite things. She didn't touch them.

Maybe, she kept thinking, when she came back from one of those other worlds, when she woke up from book dreaming, she would come back to a world where her mother wasn't dead.

She hadn't.

But she kept her mother's watch, even though it was broken. Ollie never took it off until she got home at night and then it spent its nights under her pillow. Now, as Ollie stepped into the road, she glanced down at it. 27:04, the watch said now. RUN.

Sunset at 6:03, Ollie remembered. Twenty-seven minutes sounded about right. She would have to trust it.

Maybe the advice was good too. RUN. Ollie bit a knuckle, considered the place where the driver had pointed to the little gap in the fog, the skinny path.

There was a scarecrow on her side of the road. It was peering around a tree, one garden-rake hand uplifted, wearing an old black suit. It looked like the scarecrow whose hat Brian had adjusted. That couldn't be right.

"Hey, Ollie!"

Ollie shrieked and whipped around. Coco Zintner hopped awkwardly down from the last step of the bus, right into a green puddle. Ollie glanced down at her watch. 24:08.

"Are you really leaving?" Coco asked, splashing over.

"Yes," said Ollie. The back of her neck was prickling. She found herself keeping an eye on the black-suited scarecrow.

"I'm sorry about earlier," Coco said.

"It's okay," said Ollie, but she was barely listening. She had decided. She strode toward the woods.

"Where are you going?" Coco asked, hurrying up beside her. "Why are you going so fast?"

"The woods," said Ollie, trying to sound surer than she felt. "The bus driver said, *Best get moving.* I'm moving."

Coco bit her lips. "I'm going with you. They're too mean on the bus." She showed Ollie the gummy end of her hair, and her lip quivered. "And I'm scared," she added. "This place is weird."

"Okay," Ollie said, a little relieved that *someone* was

coming with her, that she wasn't the only one afraid. Even if it was Coco Zintner. "If we go into the woods," she said, trying to make the decision more rational than it was, "we can angle back toward the farm. There's probably a short-cut in there. We'll be back before we know it."

"Look, a path!" said Coco, pointing to the gap in the trees. "That way."

Ollie had meant to go that way, but she didn't like Coco taking charge.

"Well, yes," said Ollie. "But, Coco—"

Coco didn't hear. She was already running ahead, slip-ping in puddles. Ollie followed. They crossed the grassy, overgrown space between the road and the trees. To get to the path, they had to pass the black-suited scarecrow. It did look a lot like the one Brian had pointed out earlier. Maybe they'd made two identical ones. It stood there with mist lapping around its knees, smiling blankly.

Just as they reached the first jumpy shadows of the forest, another voice yelled, "Hey, wait!"

Both girls turned around. Coco seemed to shrink into herself, but then she scowled and crossed her arms. "No boys allowed," she told Brian as he jogged across the asphalt.

Brian raised a brow. "This isn't summer camp, Cocoa Puff," he said. "Have you two completely lost it? Mr. Easton said to wait. He's coming right back. You're going to get in *so much* trouble."

"I don't think Mr. Easton is coming back," said Ollie. "It's almost dark."

"Don't call me Cocoa Puff!" cried Coco. Her blue eyes had filled up. She stroked her wounded hair.

"So what if it gets dark?" said Brian to Ollie. "Way smarter to stay inside, in one place. Someone will come tonight. But the woods will be cold—you could get lost, break an ankle, fall into the river. Don't be dumb."

Ollie knew the same things Brian knew, about what could happen to someone alone in a forest at night. He saw her hesitate. "Okay, now you're getting it," he said. "Come back to the bus. They're all in there saying you've lost it, but I don't believe it. Come back to the bus."

Ollie looked down at her watch. 18:03. RUN. The word still wavered under the watch's cracked face. "No," she said to Brian. "We have to go. Now." She headed for the woods again.

"You stay here," added Coco to Brian, shrill. She hurried after Ollie. Mist curled around the first of the tree trunks, crept softly up the road. Brian stood where they'd left him.

Ollie paused between the first of the tree trunks, turned back. "I think you should come with us, Brian. *Best get moving,* the bus driver said. I think something bad is going to happen."

Brian just stared at her like he'd never heard anything so ridiculous. The sky was the color of a wet slate roof now. Shadows seemed to be creeping out from the trees, creeping out to the noisy bus.

The driver was staring right at them out the driver's-side window, his eyes round and blank as marbles. Ollie shrank instinctively into the shadow of the trees. The driver, unsmiling, pointed once to the forest at their backs.

"Come on," Ollie whispered to Coco. "We need to go."

13

COCO DARTED INTO the trees after Ollie. The forest seemed to close around them like the bars of a cage. "I'm glad Brian didn't come," panted Coco. "He's just a—lump."

Ollie thought of Coco's notebook the day before, the two faces nestled in the perfectly shaped heart, but she didn't say anything. Coco tripped over a root and would have gone sprawling, but Ollie caught her, barely.

"You pair of idiots," said Brian, marching up behind them.

Both girls spun, still clutching each other. "I'm just following you because you're both crazy," he added. "Someone has to make sure you don't fall into the creek and die. I'll probably get a medal for it. They'll make me an Eagle Scout."

"We didn't ask you," said Coco coldly. Then she tripped again.

Brian snorted. "Only because you're complete idiots. At least City Girl here has an excuse. But you, Ollie—"

"I'm nuts, remember?" said Ollie. "Everyone says so." She quickened her pace. Some blind instinct lifted the hairs on her arms and urged her on. Coco seemed to feel it too, for she hurried along right behind.

Brian muttered, "Geez, I can't believe I'm doing this," and followed.

The path was narrow and winding, and ribbed with roots. Coco, less used to moving outdoors, kept tripping. The third time Coco lurched forward and nearly sent Ollie to the ground, she snapped, "Could you *not*?"

"Sorry," Coco said, wilting.

"Well, at least we won't get *too* far from the bus before one of you breaks an ankle," Brian said.

Ollie ignored him.

"Why do you have to be so mean?" Coco demanded of Brian.

"Mean? Are you talking about the part where I saved your lives because you ran off into a strange forest after dark?" Brian snapped back.

Coco ground her teeth. "You're just—*full of yourself*!"

Brian had his mouth open on a retort, but Ollie said, "Shut up, both of you. Either I've lost it or something's wrong. Honestly, I hope I'm crazy. But if I'm not, could we not let *the entire forest* know that we're here?"

Brian rolled his eyes, but stopped talking. Coco fell instantly quiet and tiptoed along in Ollie's wake. Ollie supposed they were trying to be quiet, but Coco made a lot of noise snapping sticks and even Brian wasn't as quiet as Ollie, who had spent years mushrooming with her mother in all kinds of terrain and weather. It would be hard to hide with this crew. Ollie wished her mom were there. She glanced once at her watch with its flickering warning. 15:56. How did her watch know?

Trees rattled overhead, masking the sound of their footsteps. The cold leaves were slimy underfoot. Coco tripped again and caught Ollie's backpack to keep herself from falling. Ollie windmilled her arms, barely keeping her own balance. She glared at Coco. *Sorry,* Coco mouthed.

Brian walked behind them grumpily. "You don't even know where you're going," he said, although he didn't talk as loud as before.

"Ollie does!" snapped Coco.

"We had to leave the bus," Ollie said. "Remember what the bus driver said? *At nightfall they'll come for the rest of you . . .*"

"I was wrong," said Brian. "You're not going to get in trouble. You're too crazy to get in trouble. Plead insanity at the hearing, that should clear things right up."

"I hope we get in trouble," said Ollie grimly. "I really hope so. Because then that would mean I'm wrong."

Brian said nothing. Cold skeleton trees clustered thick on either side. The path itself twisted and turned, going gradually downhill. There was no proper sunset, just a slow, inevitable darkness. Eventually they had to pull out their phones to see. Their flashlight apps lit the woods in pieces and made everything seem sinister and unreal. Also, Ollie thought nervously, with lights in a dark forest, they might as well have been shouting *WE'RE HERE* to anyone who cared to look.

They came to a place where the trail disappeared, and Ollie halted, uncertain.

"Where are we?" Coco whispered. Her voice sounded loud in the stillness. "It's like it's not even October anymore."

Coco was right. In Evansburg, the trees were bright with golden leaves. Here the trees were bare, the wind sharp. Brown leaves lay thick underfoot.

"The rain last night just knocked the leaves down," said Brian.

"*All* of them?" retorted Coco.

Ollie didn't say anything. She was struggling to find the path, even with their phone lights. "I think it's this way," she said, and headed off again. Coco was sticking close to Ollie, huffing and puffing and still cracking sticks under her feet.

"The way to *what?*" demanded Brian, following them, exasperated.

Ollie wished she knew, wished again that her mother

were there. The shadows were dropping faster and faster, like a net descending. *What are we doing?*

"What are we doing?" said Brian, echoing her thought. "Ollie, are you done being nuts yet?"

Her watch chimed gently against her wrist. Ollie looked down at it in startled reflex, nearly tripping on a protruding root. The display had changed. HIDE, it said. The display lit for an instant, with a flickering blue glow.

Ollie was paralyzed for a second.

The countdown said 08:00.

"I'm scared," whispered Coco.

They hurried down the path now, not talking. The leaves crunched under their feet; the trees groaned over their heads. "Where's the farm?" asked Coco. "We should have found it by now, right? Are we lost?"

HIDE.

"It's getting *dark*," said Coco.

"That tends to happen at night," Brian muttered. And then—"Who's that?" he asked suddenly, pointing. "Is that—?" It looked like a person, standing with his back to them. "Hey!" said Brian, hurrying over. "Hey, mister—"

"Brian, wait—" began Ollie.

Too late. Brian put a hand on the man's shoulder, and then yelped and jumped back. The arm flopped, the head fell sideways. It wasn't a person at all, only a scarecrow. The blank face scowled at them, hazy in the gathering dark.

"I thought it was a person," Brian whispered.

"Well," said Ollie, trying to be reasonable, to ignore her rising panic, "a scarecrow means we must be near the farm."

Coco screamed. Brian and Ollie spun. Coco stood with her hand over her mouth, pointing up at the tree trunks.

WE SEE YOU was written on a tree overhead in ragged, dripping white letters.

Below them another scarecrow leaned against the tree. There was paint on his coveralls; he was grinning ear to ear. He had no hands at all, just two flopping paintbrushes where hands should be.

The three stared at the letters a moment, disbelieving.

"What *is* that?" demanded Brian. "Some kind of weird joke? Halloween?"

"Look!" gasped Coco, pointing. Ollie followed her finger.

The first scarecrow was gone.

"I'm scared," whispered Coco. "I'm *really* scared."

A stick cracked quite nearby.

"Coco, hush," said Ollie. "Be still."

"It wasn't me," Coco replied. A pause. Then she said, in a trembling voice, "We should have stayed on the bus." She was turning in circles like a scared puppy. "Which way? I can't remember. Which way is the bus?"

"Duh," said Brian, and his voice was thin with fright. "That's what I was trying to tell you. We should have stayed on the bus. That's what they tell you to do when you're lost—stay in one place. Until they come help you."

Ollie wondered if Brian was right. Better the bus than alone in the forest with—with . . . Another stick cracked somewhere out in the darkness. Then another, louder. Closer. Their phone lights were flickering now, just like the bus lights, just like Ollie's watch.

"We can't go back right now," said Ollie. "We have to hide."

Coco and Brian hesitated.

"It will be warmer that way," Ollie improvised. Her hands had begun to shake. "It's getting colder." It was. The wind was cold as dead fingers, creeping through their sweaters and rain jackets.

"Come on," she said.

On they went, stumbling through the woods. Out in the forest came the steady cracking of sticks. "Who is *doing that*?" asked Brian, breathless and frightened. "If one of you set this up . . ."

Coco shrieked.

"What!" cried Ollie.

"Eyes," Coco whispered. "I thought I saw eyes, shining."

"Just an animal," said Brian.

Ollie didn't say anything. The spatters of rain had become the occasional snowflake, cold on her tongue and fingers. "Look," she said, stopping.

Two rocks sat leaning together, a little triangular space

between them, like a jack-o-lantern's eye. "Let's hide in there," said Ollie.

Unenthusiastic silence.

"It's too small," said Brian at last. "There might be anything in there. A snake. A skunk."

"We have to hide," said Ollie. "We have to hide *now*." 02:12, said her watch. Overhead, bare branches groaned. Ollie shone her dim phone screen into the triangle made by the leaning rocks. Damp, dark, empty. "Come on."

Brian and Coco didn't move. Behind them came a shrill *wheeee*, faint but clear through the trees. It sounded like an alarm. "What is that?" Coco whispered. Her fair hair stuck to her cheeks; she was sweating in spite of the cold.

Brian had gone still. "The alarm at the back of the bus," he said.

"*What?*" demanded Ollie.

"Mike or Phil must have opened the back door, those idiots," said Brian. Even in the weak light from their phones, Ollie could see that Brian didn't quite believe what he was saying. "There's an alarm on buses that goes off if the back door is opened."

"But," breathed Coco, "what if it *wasn't* them?"

A scream tore through the twilight. Then a whole chorus of screaming.

A bus full of kids . . .

They stared at each other.

The screams got louder.

"Oh, what is it!" cried Coco. "What—?"

Ollie's watch beeped again; it was glowing a faint blue. The countdown stood at zero.

Behind them came a *chink*, as of metal dragged along wood. Ollie thought she saw a pale patch, like a face, glimpsed between trees, then lost. *Chink*. But no, it couldn't be—it just couldn't . . .

Coco was breathing like someone trying not to scream. "I saw something moving. I saw it—just there."

Crunch, went the footsteps.

"There!" cried Brian. "I saw a face."

"It could be someone nice," said Coco, but her voice was trembling.

"It's not," said Ollie. "A nice person—a nice person would call out or something." She thought of scarecrows with trowel hands, and that thought was enough to send her onto her knees, scrabbling for the cleft between the rocks. She dove forward, found herself in a surprisingly roomy crawl space, and turned.

Up above, Coco really did scream. Brian shouted. "Coco!" Ollie cried. "Brian!" A hulking thing had come up behind them, walking on limbs that were too long and jointed in weird places. A hand—a *rake hand*—gleamed in their shaking phone lights.

"Come on!" Ollie bellowed, backing up. Coco hurtled

into the cave, bowling Ollie over. Above them, Brian screamed. Coco flipped around at once and scrabbled back to the cave entrance. "Brian!"

Ollie had an impossible glimpse of Brian lying on the ground while the black-suited scarecrow bent down toward him, rake hand reaching, as though it meant to hook itself under Brian's collar and drag him away. There were small stones in the mouth of the cave, gritty under Ollie's hands. She groped for one. The stone bounced with a *ping* off the rake, and the sound was enough to jar Brian out of his shock. "Come on, Brian, come on!" cried Coco. Brian began crawling under the rocks, Ollie let fly another stone and hit the scarecrow right below the eye.

A nightmare face turned to Ollie: stitched-on snarl, eyes like two finger-sized holes. The rake reached out again. With a desperate heave, Brian got himself into the cave and they all scrambled toward the back, panting.

A huge, straw-smelling arm thrust itself into the hole. Coco's breath sounded more like a sob. The three pressed themselves up against the back of the rock. The arm groped, almost touching Ollie's ankle. She pulled it beneath herself. Her heartbeat shook her like a rabbit in an open field.

Then the arm withdrew.

The rustling footsteps faded. A silence fell.

After a moment, Coco and Ollie and Brian turned to look at each other.

"What," said Coco, "in *hell* was that?"

Brian began to giggle. Then he began to laugh.

"What," snapped Ollie, still out of breath with fright, "is *so funny?*"

"*Alice in Wonderland,*" said Brian. "Remember? 'How do you know I'm mad?' asked Alice."

"'You must be,'" Ollie said, finishing the quotation slowly, "'or you wouldn't have come here.'"

Brian buried his face in his hands.

14

A FEW MINUTES passed. Brian wasn't laughing, and he wasn't crying; he was doing a little of both. Coco awkwardly patted his arm. Ollie was too occupied with listening to whatever was outside the cave. HIDE, her watch still said.

Finally Brian fell silent, and for a moment the only sound was three people's frightened breathing. Then Ollie said, "Listen."

They all held their breath.

Faint but clear came the sound of feet in old leaves. "Maybe that's help," said Coco. "Maybe—"

"Hush," said Brian. "It's not. Help would be talking. Calling. No one is talking."

"More scarecrows?" whispered Ollie.

Brian was nearest the opening in the rocks. Carefully, quietly, he peered out the entrance. Ollie and Coco followed, and they all managed to wedge their heads together so they could see.

No one said a word for a moment. Coco spoke first. "It—it's not people dressed up as scarecrows?"

"I don't think so," Ollie whispered.

"It has to be," insisted Coco, but her voice was a thin, scared thread.

"Quiet," said Ollie.

The scarecrows were marching. Knee up, knee down, like puppets, they marched. Wearing old secondhand clothes—plaid shirts, and funny hats, and long strings of beads—they clomped through the leaves.

Hooked onto their curving garden-rake hands, stumbling in a silent, straggling line, came the sixth graders of Ben Withers Middle School.

"Where're they taking them?" Brian asked. His voice shook.

Why don't they run away? Ollie thought.

Brian gasped—"Phil!" He spoke too loudly.

Ollie wrenched around, but Coco had already flung herself forward and put a hand over Brian's mouth. "Quiet, Brian!" she snapped.

Phil didn't even look up. But one of the scarecrows had stopped. It raised its head. Sniff. Shuffle. Sniff again.

The others were marching off. *Swish* went their feet.

But the one scarecrow stayed, looking around with its stitched-on eyes.

None of the three under the rocks dared to breathe.

The scarecrow was going here and there, jerkily, like a dog that had lost a scent. It came right up to their tiny cave. All three flinched and hunkered down. A scarecrow arm thrust itself into the hole. This arm ended in a trowel. Ollie and Brian and Coco pressed themselves into the rock.

Then the hand was gone. The scarecrow marched away, following the others. The sound of footsteps faded.

"Why didn't they run?" whispered Coco.

Ollie didn't know.

"We have to help the others," Brian breathed. "We have to—" He looked like he was going to go charging out into the night.

Ollie got hold of the back of Brian's jacket. "Do you think we could help them? Right now?" Ollie demanded. "You'll only get caught by a scarecrow yourself, and how would that help anyone?"

"Ollie's right," said Coco. "You can't do anything while it's nighttime. They'll just get you too."

Brian flinched, but the crazy impulse seemed to pass. He gathered his knees to his chest and didn't say a word.

"We have to stay here until morning," Ollie said. "Tomorrow—we'll figure out what to do."

No one said anything else, but after a minute, Coco began to cry.

"Come on," said Ollie. "Don't cry. Tomorrow we can make a plan. Tomorrow."

Ollie could hear muffled sounds, as though Brian were crying in the dark as well but didn't want them to know.

"What is this place?" Coco whispered.

Ollie had no idea. The night had gone very quiet. There was no noise at all except for their breathing in the little cave. They were all jammed together, but no one suggested getting out. Ollie was sure she would be awake all night. The space was really uncomfortable. Pitch-black.

But she fell asleep anyway.

She dreamed, as she nearly always did, of fire in a gray field. But this time, ranged around the edges of the field were scarecrows, watching the metal and plastic and grass burn. Ollie could see her mother, there in the wreckage, and she tried to run but a scarecrow had her by the hair, had hooked its rake hand in, and she could only writhe helplessly as the fire grew and grew and grew . . .

Ollie woke up with a shriek to find daylight trickling into the mouth of the cave.

15

"WHAT!" SNAPPED BRIAN, jerking awake himself. "Ollie, what?"

Ollie was still breathing hard. Even though it was cold, she had fear-sweat on her face. She wished she could brush her teeth. "Nothing," she said. "Just a dream."

"You were screaming," said Coco. She looked as though she'd been awake before Ollie yelled. "Must have been a pretty bad dream."

"Yeah," said Ollie. She didn't want to say anything about her dreams. She sat up—there was just headroom for it—and looked around her. Flat morning light trickled into their little cave. They had slept in one tangled and uncomfortable pile. Ollie's skin felt clammy; her leg was asleep.

Brian sat up and said, "I was really hoping last night was a nightmare. I was looking forward to waking up in bed."

"Me too," Ollie admitted.

"But we're here," said Brian. "Not a nightmare."

"No," said Ollie.

"How'd you know, Ollie?" asked Brian. "You believed the bus driver, you went out into the woods—and all this happened. You were right. But how could you have guessed?"

"It's a long story," said Ollie. "I'll tell you, but I have to pee first. And I'm hungry."

They all looked nervously at the mouth of their little cave.

"Do you think they're gone?" Coco asked. Cautiously, she poked her head out. "I can't hear anything." She crawled all the way out, stood up slowly. "Seems okay," she called.

Ollie, feeling nervous, crept out of the cave, trying to stamp feeling back into her leg. Brian emerged in her wake, breathing on his cold fingers.

Ollie didn't know what she was expecting. Some sign of their kidnapped classmates? At least a stray glove here and there? But there was nothing except for churned-up leaves and their three selves. The sky was the color of snow but without the sparkle. The air was chilly and damp. Ollie wished she'd worn warmer clothes.

Coco was nowhere to be seen.

Ollie turned in a circle. "Coco, where—?"

"I'm up here." Coco had scrambled atop the boulders that had formed their little rock sanctuary. "No sign of the others."

Ollie was impressed. The rocks were steep and slippery. Brian whistled. "How'd you get up there?"

Coco peered down. She looked, Ollie saw with surprise, happier than she had ever looked at school. "I was junior rock-climbing champion back home. I never climbed outside, just in the gym, but I liked it. I had friends and everything. But people here only climb outside and my mom says it's not safe. I haven't climbed in a while. I miss it." Coco giggled, a strange sound in that grim forest. "If only Mom could see me now."

"Can you see anything up there?" Ollie asked.

Coco on the rocks was pretty confident for a tiny person who was so clumsy on the ground. She turned in a slow circle, squinting.

"Trees," she said. "Trees, and—" Coco paused. "The river!" she cried triumphantly. "Just there. I can see it shine. And something red. The farm! We're not lost!"

"Lethe Creek," said Brian. "And Misty Valley. We should go down to the farm. Get help. Do your phones work? Mine still doesn't."

Ollie checked. NO SERVICE, it said, with dashes where the time should have been. "I don't have much battery either," she said. She turned her phone off again. Might as well save what was left. Brian was doing the same.

Brian was right. They should head down to the farm. Ollie glanced at her watch. RIVER, it said, and a new countdown had started. 06:37:41. Coco skidded down the side of the boulder and landed on her feet. "My phone doesn't work either," she said. "I checked this morning. Where do you think the others—went?" Coco shivered suddenly.

"No idea. We have to go get help," said Brian. "The police will have sniffer dogs and things." He went over to a tree in the direction Coco had pointed and pulled off a strip of bark, marking the direction of the farm. *He must actually be in the Boy Scouts,* Ollie thought, remembering the Eagle Scout comment the night before.

"That might take too long," Coco pressed. "They were kidnapped by scarecrows! We have to help them." Apparently Coco held no grudges for the gum, or the notebook, or a dozen other things. Ollie felt a reluctant admiration for Coco Zintner.

"Right. About that," said Brian. "Ollie, how did you know? About getting away and hiding, and the scarecrows and everything? If it weren't for you we'd . . ." He trailed off.

"Yeah," Coco chimed in. "Thanks for saving us."

Ollie hadn't thought of it like that before. "You're welcome," she said awkwardly. "Um—I didn't know. Not exactly. But—hang on, I have to pee." She went behind a tree, like on a camping trip. When she came back, Coco was looking like she wanted to do the same but was really embarrassed. "Go on," said Ollie, amused. "It's better than a gas station bathroom."

132

Coco went and came back fast. "No, it's not," she said, sneezing. "It's cold and wet."

Ollie grinned and plunged into the story of stealing *Small Spaces*, of Beth, Caleb, Jonathan, and the smiling man, of the strange similarities between Misty Valley and Smoke Hollow. Of the bus driver's warning. She pulled the book out, let them read the epigraph.

"So let me get this straight," said Brian, when she'd finished. "Jonathan made a deal with this guy—the smiling man. Who brought his brother back to life. Then Jonathan disappeared. And then his brother disappeared. And *then* the schoolhouse-fire kids disappeared. Assuming they weren't burned to death. So—what, have we disappeared now?"

"Maybe," said Ollie. Put so clearly, she wasn't sure. "I mean—the book was right about the mist rising and stuff. And about avoiding large places at night. If we hadn't found that cave, we'd have been grabbed too."

"Is this all because of the smiling man, then?" whispered Coco. "Who is he? Do you think—do you think he's around?"

A hundred years later? "I don't know," said Ollie slowly, wishing she could say, *Of course not.* "Maybe—well, the bus driver said, *His people are coming.* Those'd be the scarecrows, I guess. Maybe they—work for the smiling man?"

"Or could all be just coincidence," said Brian impatiently. "In math, when two angles coincide, they fit together

133

perfectly," Ollie said. "All of this has to fit together too. Somehow."

A small frown appeared between Coco's pinkish eyebrows. "But the schoolhouse-fire kids didn't make a bargain or summon the smiling man or anything, did they? Neither did we. So, why? Why *us*?"

"I don't know," said Ollie.

"Deliver us from evil," Brian said suddenly, and crossed himself. The girls looked at him. "What?" he said. "I'm not a *good* Catholic but maybe God is listening."

"Maybe," said Coco. She shivered again. "I wonder who else is listening? I hope not the scarecrows."

They all glanced around at the silent forest. They could see no one but themselves.

"Well," said Ollie, "if *we* have disappeared, can we assume that this place is—somewhere else? Like a horrible sort of Narnia? Not our world at all? And when the mist rises, you fall through the door? Maybe the scarecrows sort of exist in both worlds? The bus driver said something like that. That they're only dangerous here at night, something about them being partly in the sunshine world during the day." Even to Ollie it sounded far-fetched.

"Narnia?" said Coco, sounding puzzled. "What's Narnia?"

"The Pevensies go to Narnia through the wardrobe, when it was under the control of the White Witch," said

Brian. "That's why it was always winter but never Christmas. Don't you read?"

"I don't like novels," said Coco with dignity. "I like books that tell you about real things. So you think the smiling man is the White Witch? He controls this place? Is that what you mean?"

Ollie hadn't thought of it that way. They didn't even know if the smiling man was real.

"Someone has to be doing this," Coco continued. "Maybe the scarecrows are like—like robots and someone is pulling the strings. A White Witch. The smiling man."

"Robots don't have strings. That's marionettes," said Brian.

"*Whatever,*" said Coco.

Then Brian said slowly, "If you're right, then maybe there's not help waiting on the farm. Maybe that's where the—the *puppet master*, is and that's worse."

"But if there *are* any answers, they have to be on the farm," Coco said. "Not here in the woods. And," she added practically, "we can't just stay here. We'll starve."

"Not today," said Ollie. She pulled out her lunch box. She was getting hungry anyway. Three quarters of a huge turkey sandwich, a chocolate chip muffin, carrot sticks, a bag of homemade granola, a slice of pumpkin pie from the farm, and peanut butter cookies all lay nestled in her big unicorn lunch box, and Ollie had never in her life been more grateful for her dad's overpacking. "I have this," she said. "We should eat the turkey sandwich soon, anyway. The meat won't keep."

Coco was rummaging in her own backpack. She pulled out a large bag of trail mix. "I have this."

They both looked at Brian. He scraped a foot in the leaves. "I ate my snacks yesterday," he said, a little shamefaced. "I got hungry on the bus."

Boys. Ollie and Coco had the same thought at the same time. They looked at each other and Ollie almost laughed. "Right," she said. "We should eat and then make a plan." That's what her mom had always said on hiking trips. *If you're ever lost, think of your basic needs first. Are you hungry, are you thirsty, are you hurt?* Ollie wished for the millionth time that her mother were there.

"You can't eat all *our* food," said Coco to Brian, holding her trail mix a little defensively. "We have to make it last."

Brian looked offended. "I'm not *dumb*," he said.

"Hey, we shouldn't argue here," said Ollie to both of them. "We need to keep our heads."

Coco relented. "I'm hungry too." It was kind of an apology.

"I won't eat all the food," said Brian, still cranky.

Ollie passed around hand sanitizer, and handed out

pieces of sandwich. "I know it's not very breakfast-ish," she said half-apologetically, but Brian and Coco were already eating.

"This is fantastic," said Brian, munching his sandwich. "Like Thanksgiving in brown bread."

"My dad baked the bread himself," said Ollie, trying to suppress a surge of longing. On winter weekends, her dad would get up before anyone else and get the fire going. Then he would drink coffee, watch the news, and start mixing pancake batter for breakfast. Gingerbread, buttermilk, sometimes cornmeal. The smell would wake Ollie up and she would pad downstairs just in time to catch the first pancakes coming off the griddle. Then she and her mom would play chess while her dad flipped new pancakes and egged them both on.

Her dad was probably frantic, Ollie thought. He would have spent the evening waiting for a bus that never arrived. People would be looking for them. They would be searching the farm, checking the road in between, looking for wrecks. They might find the bus. But Ollie was pretty sure they wouldn't find any people. The mist had risen, and they had disappeared. Like Caleb and Jonathan. Like the schoolhouse-fire kids.

But there had to be a way out. There had to be.

Coco was eating her quarter sandwich in tiny bites. Brian

had already finished his. Ollie sipped from her water bottle, then passed it around. Coco and Brian gulped the water. Being terrified makes your mouth dry. "Hey, slow down," said Ollie. "The water might have to last the day." She wasn't going to think about the night. Surely, they'd be home by then.

"Sorry," said Coco, handing the bottle back. It was more than half empty. Ollie tried not to worry about it. They couldn't do anything just then anyway. She clasped her lunch box again, put it away.

"So," she said. "What now?"

"We need a way out," said Brian.

"What about the others?" cried Coco.

"We need to get help first," said Brian.

"What are we going to say if we do find help?" asked Ollie. "Our classmates were kidnapped by evil-demon scarecrows, please help us?"

"Maybe not exactly that," admitted Brian. "But what else are we going to do? We can't help anyone if we're dead, and Ollie, your water bottle is not going to last forever."

"You're not wrong," said Ollie slowly. She glanced down at her watch: 05:29:37. And RIVER.

"Let's head to the creek, then," she said. "It runs by the farm, it's a source of water, and it's downhill from here, so it means an easier day."

All the while she was making reasonable arguments,

a thought was creeping in around the edges of her awareness. Was her mother's broken watch helping them?

"I think Ollie's right," said Coco. "We can't stay here. And maybe there'll be people there. Or a clue. Something."

Ollie broke in hurriedly. "I think you're right." She wondered if she should tell Brian and Coco about her watch. About what she thought it might mean. But she couldn't. She was afraid of seeing pity in their eyes. Sympathy face. Of having them tell her that hope had clouded her judgment. That her mom wasn't really talking to her.

"Even a featherbrain is right occasionally," said Coco, a bit sourly.

Brian grinned. "It's just because you're so little and pinkish that people think that."

"*You* think that," said Coco.

"Not anymore," said Brian.

There was a slightly awkward pause. "I don't have a better idea," said Brian.

"Then let's do it," said Ollie. She picked up her backpack.

"Okay," said Coco, grabbing her own backpack. "But I really hope you guys know what you're doing."

Nope, not at all, Ollie thought. She looked up at Brian and saw him having the same thought. She grinned suddenly. You can't, she decided, be super scared for very long before you start just laughing or crying.

And indeed, Brian snorted and then they were both laughing, and Coco was staring grumpily between them. Her pink-pale hair stuck up like she was a fuzzy baby bird, and somehow that made Ollie laugh even harder.

A sudden wind picked up and raced through the trees, bringing a splat of rain. The cold drops slid under her jacket and the collar of her sweater. Ollie calmed down.

Brian, looking from side to side, set off downhill. Coco followed, skidding on leaves. Ollie went last, trying not to look too often over her shoulder.

16

THEY DIDN'T SEE any other people at all, and they were thirsty by noon, but they had to make the water bottle last. All kinds of hazards lay under the leaves: mud and puddles and roots to trip you. They had to pick their way along, skidding on the wet leaves. Ollie wished she had her hiking boots. Rain boots were not the best.

But Coco was worse off. She was wearing canvas shoes and cotton socks and wasn't used to the cold, not like Ollie and Brian. An hour in, Ollie saw that Coco's lips were becoming an unpleasant sort of pale color. Ollie took off her rainbow hat and jammed it onto Coco's head.

Coco opened her mouth, tripped, caught herself, and said, "Thanks—Olivia."

Ollie said, "You're welcome. But seriously, call me Ollie."

On they walked. The sky did not change. The trees did not change. Ollie would have wondered if they were going in circles, except that she and Brian were taking turns to blaze trees they'd passed with a gold marker from Coco's backpack.

A few times Ollie thought she heard a rustle in the leaves, like a bird or a squirrel. When she looked, nothing was there. But it gave her a creepy feeling, like something was slipping quietly along behind them.

They sipped water and ate a handful of Coco's trail mix, chewing slowly to make it last.

Brian stayed in front and Ollie stayed in back. They did it on purpose, keeping Coco in the middle. They didn't trust her to not get lost.

"Guys!" Brian yelled from ahead of them. "I think I see something!"

Both girls hurried to catch up. Coco, Ollie thought critically, looked like she was tripping only every ten steps now. An improvement.

The trees ended; they found themselves on the edge of a clearing. In the middle of the clearing was a tidy white house. Ollie stared like it was a mirage. Of all the things she was expecting in this creepy forest, a cozy cabin was not one of them. Ollie smelled woodsmoke and laundry and something spicy.

Coco's eyes were shining. "It's okay! We're not lost anymore! We can call my dad from here! Hellooo!" Coco yelled.

Someone waved in answer. A lady stood in the yard, hanging laundry. She wore a baggy old dress, her hair a friendly brown braid down her back. Coco and Brian ran forward. Ollie followed, frowning. There was something weird about the scene but she didn't quite know what it was.

The woman caught sight of them. "Look at this!" she cried, smiling. "Three of them, as I live and breathe! At lunchtime too! Are you hungry?"

"Yes! Thank you!" cried Coco.

Ollie still hung back. She was thinking of Hansel and Gretel, and the witch's gingerbread cottage. But the lady seemed—nice. Ordinary. And she was a person! Not a scarecrow. Her eyes weren't white but reassuringly blue. "Come in, my ducks," she said. "You look cold."

Coco was already at the gate of the cottage garden. Ollie still hesitated. Brian looked back. "Ollie?" he said. "What is it?"

Ollie didn't know. She just knew that something was weird. She looked down at her watch: 03:10:49, said the countdown. And now there was a word, FOOD. FOOD but crossed out. What did *that* mean? No food? Now Ollie wondered if she should have explained about her watch, so she could ask the others what they thought. It was true they didn't have that much food. And if the lady was offering . . .

The lady was bustling Coco through the door.

"What do you think, Ollie?" Brian asked.

Ollie was still frowning, trying to say what was bothering her. "She's hanging her laundry," Ollie replied slowly. "On a day like this?" She gestured toward the damp forest. "It will never dry." Ollie thought some more, looking around. "And she lives here? But there's no road."

There wasn't. Just a thin track through the forest. Who lived in a place with no road?

"No generator," said Brian, realizing. "No power lines, even. Okay, that is weird. Does your phone work here?" Brian had already pulled out his. "No Wi-Fi either."

Brian and Ollie looked at each other. "It's like it's not a real house at all," said Brian. "What real house has no road *and* no electricity? Are we still in the bad Narnia? How do we tell?"

"I don't know," Ollie said.

"Well—it might be okay?" said Brian. "Even if it's not, one lady can't be a match for the three of us, can she? Maybe she'll have some answers."

Ollie looked down at her watch again. ~~FOOD~~, said the digital display.

"It might be all right," said Ollie. "But we should be really careful."

Cautiously they crossed the cottage garden and stepped into the lady's neat white house. It was bright and tidy and cheerful and warm. A woodstove sat next to a wood rack in the corner. Ollie, despite herself, sighed in relief when the hot air from the stove touched her chilled face.

The house was old-fashioned. A big old cuckoo clock ticked away to itself. The stove gave off a soft, golden firelight, and there was an oil lamp lit on the table, like the pewter one her dad had and lit for special occasions. The woman had opened her oven, was peering into its depths. Ollie had a glimpse of a rich brown cake puffing up in its pan. It smelled fantastic.

"Nearly done," said the woman. She banged the oven door shut and rubbed her back. "What brings you to these parts?" she asked. She had a full kettle on the stove and went to a cupboard and got out what looked like tea leaves pressed into a square. She began crumbling the tea into six cups.

Why six cups, Ollie wondered. *Who are the other two for?*

"Are you taken on to work at the farm for the summer?" the woman asked. She frowned at the kids' backpacks and jackets, at Ollie's rain boots. "You're dressed strangely for it."

"No," Coco said in her best impress-adults voice. "We only went to the farm for the day. We have to go to school usually. But if you don't mind, we're looking for—"

The woman turned around suddenly, hands on her hips, and shook a teaspoon at Coco. "Well, look who's high and mighty now," she said. "No work, just because

145

you have to go to school! Well, I'll have you know both my boys work *and* go to school, and they are the better for it!" Her face turned red.

"Sorry," said Coco. She was wearing her most angelic face, the kind that made adults pat her head. "We didn't mean to offend you. Do you have a phone? I want to call my mom."

Instantly the woman's face softened. "No, pretty child, I am sure you meant no disrespect. And I do sometimes get it muddled—summer and winter—winter and summer. Funny how the seasons run together. I depend on my boys to tell me the day. They're due back soon. If we all sit down together and eat gingerbread, they'll be back before we know it."

Coco and Ollie and Brian looked at each other. After a moment, Coco and Brian sat down, warily, but Ollie stayed standing.

"Yes," the old woman went on, "they will be home soon. Very soon." She bustled with the tea and gingerbread.

She whispered to herself as she worked. "Mother's waiting. She's waiting—" The lady opened the oven and took out the gingerbread. "Sometimes it seems like I do more waiting than not, these days."

The gingerbread came plunk down on the middle of the table. The woman cut six generous slices and heaped each plate high. She smiled at her visitors. "There, dears," she said. "Isn't this nice?"

"Oh yes," said Coco. "Very nice. I'm Coco Zintner. This is Brian Battersby and Olivia Adler. Thank you so much for the food. What's your name?"

"I'm Mrs. Webster," said the lady cheerfully. "Though everyone calls me Cathy."

Brian's glance flew to Ollie's. Coco, intent on being angelic, hadn't really registered the name.

"Do you know anything about the scarecrows?" Brian asked the woman.

Cathy was putting more logs on the fire. "Scarecrows?" she asked vaguely. "What, out in the corn?"

Cathy Webster is dead, Ollie thought. *Her bones are in the graveyard.*

"They're so festive in the fall, with pumpkins," Cathy went on.

Ollie broke in sharply, "Your sons, when are they coming?"

"Soon," said Cathy, and smiled. "I'm keeping the stove hot for them. They will have baths by the fire, and good hot tea."

Both Brian and Coco had picked up their steaming gingerbread as they listened.

"What are their names?" whispered Ollie.

The old lady looked surprised. "Why, Jonathan," she said. "And Caleb, of course, my—"

A *rap* came sharp on the window. Ollie spun. In each window was a face. Two smiling scarecrow faces, two

147

scarecrows dressed in old-fashioned black suits. Ollie screamed, short and sharp, just as Brian and Coco gagged together. It was not gingerbread they had bitten into. It was some foul thing, moldy and dry; they each spat out a mouthful of rotten dust.

They were on their feet, hemmed in, and then a bony hand wrapped around Ollie's wrist. Ollie screamed again. The woman didn't look alive anymore. Her face was shriveled, her mouth fallen in. "Tell them to come in," Cathy whispered. "Please—tell them to come in. They come to the door, and I can hear them crying in the night. But they never come in. Tell them I've been waiting in this place— how long? I don't remember anymore. Long and long and long and . . ."

The fire was out in the oven. The shutter rattled. The china was all covered with dust; it was icy cold.

Ollie wrenched free. "We have to go!" she cried.

"There are scarecrows right outside!" snapped Brian.

"We have to risk it," said Ollie. "The bus driver said they're only dangerous at night, remember?"

"The bus driver who *brought us here*?" demanded Coco.

The woman had hurried to the window. "My boys, my dear ones, *please*." She was fumbling at the window, and beyond her were the blank, smiling faces of the scarecrows.

"Come *on*," said Ollie. The three of them ran, tripping over the threshold. Two scarecrows stood outside, one at each window. Somehow, they were not looking into the house anymore, but were watching the kids run, still smiling their wide smiles. The laundry was rotting on the line, the shutter banging and banging and *banging* . . .

Ollie, Coco, and Brian dashed into the woods, dodging trees, wild with panic, sure the scarecrows were marching behind them in steady pursuit, while their dead mother wailed in her cold house.

17

OLLIE CAUGHT ONE of her duck-printed rain boots under a tree root and went down with a cry, ripping her jeans and smearing herself with mud. Brian stopped when she yelled, and Coco tripped over her, knocking the wind out of them both.

"Come on!" cried Brian, while Ollie and Coco lay wheezing on the ground. He was faster than either of them, what with the hockey and everything, but he waited for them, panting. "We have to go!"

Ollie got to her hands and knees, still heaving for breath. She looked around. "No one's chasing us," she said. "We'll only exhaust ourselves. You okay, Coco?"

"I think so," she said, rubbing her knees. Brian was scanning the woods, but Ollie had been right—there was no one in the woods but them.

Almost no one. Ollie jumped with a little cry. "Look!"

Written on a tree trunk a few paces away, in sloppy white letters, were two words.

STILL WATCHING

Below, a new scarecrow, wearing an old-fashioned flowered dress, leaned against a tree. Both her hands were paintbrushes.

"Come on, come *on!*" cried Coco, scrambling up.

"Hang on," said Ollie. "If the scarecrows could get us in daylight, they would have back at Cathy Webster's house. It's like the bus driver said."

She walked up to the scarecrow. It didn't move. She poked it. It felt like an ordinary scarecrow. Cloth over straw.

"Are you crazy?" Coco demanded. "*They're* watching *us*! If they can't grab us during the day, all they have to do is watch us until dark!"

"Were those *scarecrows* really Caleb and Jonathan?" asked Brian. "Or did that crazy ghost just think they were?"

"I don't know," said Ollie. She found herself hoping Cathy was wrong. But she wasn't sure. Jonathan had promised to serve the smiling man. And the bus driver had called the scarecrows *his servants*.

"Why can't they get us during the day?" Brian asked.

"Something about them being only partway in the sunshine world," said Ollie. "They're weaker. The bus driver said. I dunno."

"Sunshine world?" said Brian. "So they're in both

151

worlds? Even though we aren't? Wonder if they know a way for us to get home?"

"Also, what was Cathy doing here?" Coco piped up. "If she's the lady from your book, Ollie."

Ollie didn't know that either. She hoped neither of the others could see her shiver.

To reassure herself, Ollie looked down at her watch. The countdown read 02:50:45. They still had a while until sundown. And the old word—RIVER. Okay, that was what ~~FOOD~~ had meant. Don't eat the food. Duh. She opened her mouth to tell Brian and Coco about her watch, then closed it again.

"Do you hear that?" asked Brian suddenly.

They all went still, listening.

"Is that running water?" asked Coco.

"Lethe Creek," said Brian. "Finally. Come on, if you've had enough playing chicken with that creepy thing, Ollie, let's go. I'm thirsty."

They hurried on, not without several backward glances.

Ahead of them came the sound of roaring water. They could just see it shining through the trees when Brian halted and said, "Hold up a minute. Ollie, you're bleeding."

Ollie hadn't noticed. She looked down and saw a good-sized gash on her knee. "I've got a Band-Aid in my bag," Brian said. "Let's clean it off at least. The last thing you need now is tetanus."

"Tetanus," said Ollie, "will just have to get in line

behind dehydration, exposure, starving, and, oh right, kidnapping by evil scarecrows." But she didn't protest when Brian dug into his bag and got out a teeny first-aid kit.

"They'll definitely make you an Eagle Scout for this," said Coco, impressed.

Brian looked proud of himself. He dug out an alcohol pad, some Neosporin, and a Snoopy Band-Aid, and passed them to Ollie. She wiped away the blood, dabbed on some ointment, stuck the Snoopy on, and felt strangely better. While they were at it, Coco changed the Band-Aid on her chin and Ollie changed the one on the back of Brian's head. They all felt better after, not because they had such bad cuts or anything, but more because the last twenty-four hours had been so full of mysteries and impossible problems and being scared. It was a relief to deal with an ordinary problem, like a scraped knee.

"Thanks, Brian," said Ollie, meaning it.

Brian looked a little embarrassed. "Don't mention it."

"Let's go before the scarecrows come!" Coco said. "Or the ghost." She was shifting from foot to foot.

Ollie had a sudden mental image of a skull-headed woman floating toward them, feet not quite touching the ground, with her two scarecrow sons lurching along behind. She shivered and got to her feet. They started off downhill toward the roaring of the water.

Brian was looking worried. "That gingerbread," he said. "I—it wasn't like Persephone, was it?"

Coco looked puzzled, but Ollie got it. "Persephone ate food in the underworld after being abducted by Hades," she explained. "As a consequence of eating there, she had to spend part of every year in the underworld forever."

Now Coco looked scared. "I don't think I ate the gingerbread," she said. "I think I spat it out."

"Me too," said Brian. "I spat it out. We shouldn't have eaten it in the first place. But I was hungry."

"It's probably okay," said Ollie. "Besides, we have to drink the water, and that comes from here too." She shook her empty bottle for emphasis and pointed to the foaming creek. Now Brian and Coco looked *very* uncertain. "There might be weird rules to this place that we don't know about," said Ollie. "But dehydration is real."

"So is dysentery," said Brian. "Lethe Creek goes past how many farms?"

"In the real world it does," said Ollie. "But here? Have you seen *any* animals? Like, any?"

"I thought I saw eyes the first night," said Coco. "Green eyes. Like a raccoon or something. But maybe I was wrong."

"I thought I heard an animal padding around while we were walking," Brian admitted. "But I didn't see anything."

"We're still going to have to risk the creek," said Ollie. "We won't get far without water." While Brian and Coco waited, she went down the slippery bank of Lethe Creek. The water looked colder and darker and faster here. It whispered against the rocks like it had a voice. Ollie hurriedly filled her bottle and went back to the others. "Here," she said. "Have a sip, and a snack will make us all feel better." Ollie got the chocolate chip muffin from her lunch box. She broke it into three pieces and passed it around.

They all munched for a few minutes. "Man," said Brian, looking happier. "Your dad really can bake."

"Yeah," said Ollie, and felt tears pricking her eyes. "He knits too. He knitted my socks."

"Don't be sad, Ollie," Coco said at once. "You'll see him again. We all will." Coco lifted her chin. "After we beat those scarecrows."

"You tell 'em, Tiny," said Brian, and Coco glared.

Ollie grinned and took a cautious sip from her bottle. The water was cold and a little metallic. Brian said, "I really hope you're right," drank, and passed the bottle to Coco.

"Is this hell?" Coco whispered, small-voiced, after she drank.

"Nope," said Ollie. "It definitely isn't. Hell wouldn't be so wet. Besides, we didn't do anything bad. Also we're not dead."

She wasn't really religious herself, and Brian looked doubtful, but he said, "Don't worry, Tiny."

"Don't call me Tiny," said Coco. "I'm normal. You're just—big."

Ollie barely heard their sniping. She had remembered something. "When I met her by the creek, Linda Webster was talking about making a bargain."

"With the smiling man, maybe?" Brian asked. "Just like Jonathan? Her soul for—?"

Ollie's lips pressed together. "Not her own soul. Ours. That's why we ended up here. One busload of kids, signed, sealed, delivered, for—whatever he gave her."

"That doesn't seem fair," said Brian. "No one asked us."

Ollie thought of a torn-up field in the rain. "A lot of things aren't fair," she said. "What now?" She glanced down at her watch. HOUSE, it said.

To their right, a narrow, covered footbridge crossed the creek, high above the racing water. On the other side of the creek lay cornfields, a vegetable garden, berry patches, hog pens, a cattle shed. Only it wasn't a tidy collection of buildings like yesterday. This farm was old, worn. They couldn't see any signs of life, but that didn't mean there weren't any.

There were a *lot* of scarecrows. They jutted out of the field; they clustered around the house. "You sure they aren't dangerous before dark?" Brian muttered.

"Mostly sure," said Ollie.

"Do you think there are any answers over there?" Brian asked. "'Cause honestly, that's a lot of scarecrows, and there's not *that* much daylight left. Maybe we should stay on this side of the creek."

"Yes," said Ollie. "I think there are answers over there." She took a deep breath. "So, guys, there's something I haven't told you. And it might be just my imagination, but . . ."

Ollie explained about her watch.

Neither Brian nor Coco said anything for a moment. Then Coco said, logically, "Well, if Cathy Webster's here, then I'd bet anything your mom is here too. Helping us." She smiled. "That makes me feel better."

"Me too," said Brian.

"Really?" said Ollie, enormously relieved.

"Yup," said Brian. "Guess we're going to the house. Coco?"

"Let's go look," said Coco nervously. "But we have to find somewhere to hide before dark."

They headed for the footbridge. As they walked, Ollie saw that Coco's stupid heart-printed sneakers were soaked. She'd probably had cold feet for the whole day but hadn't complained, not once.

Coco is all right, Ollie thought.

Aloud she said, "Come on. An hour until sunset."

"It seems like the day should have been longer," said Brian. "Yesterday too. It got dark *really* soon after we left the bus."

"Bad Narnia," said Ollie. "I guess it's darker here." Below them, Lethe Creek ran fast and cold in the evening light. A mist was just gathering in the cornfield.

18

OKAY, MAYBE MS. WEBSTER *traded us to the smiling man, and so we ended up here. But how do we get out of here? How do we get everyone out of here?*

Ollie didn't know. But she felt, urgently, that she *ought* to know, that there was a piece of the puzzle that had escaped her. It was one thing solving puzzles in math class. But now their lives were on the line and Ollie didn't have a clue.

Brian and Coco had gotten to the opening of the covered footbridge. They stopped. Ollie caught up to them. The covered bridge, which had looked okay from far away, was actually pretty rotten, its planking splintering into the creek below. They could see the water through the holes.

Coco said, unhappily, "I didn't know there would be so many scarecrows on the farm. Or that the bridge would look like that."

"We have to hurry," said Ollie. "So we can get there before dark. The bridge isn't that bad."

A dubious silence. The entrance to the bridge looked like a hungry black mouth.

"Okay," said Brian, taking a deep breath. "Great." Without another word, he started across. The timber groaned under his feet. Once he slipped and grabbed a beam so he wouldn't fall into the water. Coco said, "Oh, *God*," and followed him across.

Ollie hung back. Despite her bravado, she hated heights. Yes, this bridge wasn't *that* high, but the timbers were soft and black, slimy and splintery, and Ollie could see the gray water rushing below.

Coco was already at the middle of the bridge. Brian got to the other side and turned to watch the girls. Coco put a foot through a rotten plank, squeaked, and skipped over to the next plank. It groaned under her weight. "I'm scared," she said so that only Ollie could hear.

Ollie was still on the far side. She forced herself to take a step. It was that or stay alone on this side of the bridge with nowhere to hide and night coming on.

Step. The rotten wood bent under her feet. Step. Don't look down.

She hadn't always hated heights. Her mother used to take her flying on weekends. Ollie had loved it, the rumble and soar of the plane, bright sunshine all around, clouds like giant fish, the ground falling away.

Step.

At the funeral, they had her mother's casket closed. It was easy to believe that her mother wasn't in there at all, that she was just—at a conference or something—and would come home any minute, kiss Ollie's dad, and say, *Good adventures today, Olivia?*

Easier to imagine that than to imagine the ground coming up, big bigger biggest. Falling.

Ollie was halfway across the bridge, high above the creek, and memory had paralyzed her. *Mom fell. I could fall.*

"Ollie!" Coco called. "Ollie, come on!"

She had to move. She had to. But she couldn't.

"Ollie, hurry!"

Ollie tried to lift her foot. Failed.

Voices at the other end of the bridge. Arguing. She could barely hear them over the roaring in her own head.

The water gurgled below. In her head was the rush and surge of ground coming up to meet her. She couldn't see anything else.

Then a face thrust itself between her and memory. A ridiculously pretty face, with angelic blue eyes and pinkish hair. Coco. Hot Cocoa, Cocoa Puff. She of the dumb name and the ridiculous hair. She who cried all the time. Coco was taking Ollie's hands, standing light as—as a climber on rotten wood.

"Come on, Ollie," she said. "Come on. Step. Just one step. We can't stay here."

Ollie stepped.

Coco stepped back. "Now another one. Come on."

Ollie took another step. She wasn't falling. She wasn't going to fall. Coco's blue eyes promised it, and her thin hands. Strong hands, Ollie realized. Coco didn't cry because she was weak. Coco cried because she felt things. Ollie never cried because she didn't feel things. Not anymore. Not really. She tried not to feel things.

Step and step. One more.

And then the bridge ended. Ollie stumbled off, blind, and realized that she was crying now, hands over her face. She knelt on the stony path at the mouth of the covered bridge and she cried. She didn't even know, really, what she was crying for, whether it was from fear, tiredness, or for her mom at last.

"It's okay," Coco said. "Don't feel bad. When I went climbing the first time, I froze at the top of a wall. They had to pry me down. Please don't cry."

"I'm not," said Ollie weakly.

Then she scrubbed her hands down her face. "I'm not," she repeated, more firmly. She stood up. "I'm okay now. Thanks, Coco. You saved me back there."

Coco beamed. "Don't mention it."

Ollie looked around. "Where's Brian?"

Startled, Coco said, "I don't know. He was just—"

"Guys, get over here now!" Brian's shout came from the direction of the vegetable garden.

Ollie and Coco hurried up the sloping path. The first of the scarecrows stood right on the edge of the fenced-in dead garden, head a little flopped to one side. Brian was standing in front of it, his hand over his mouth.

"What is it?" said Coco.

"That scarecrow," Ollie said, panting a little. "Is—does it look familiar?"

"Yes," Brian whispered. "Because it's wearing Phil's clothes. Because that's Phil's hat and Phil's hair and kind of Phil's face—if it were sewn on. That's Phil."

"No," said Coco. "Or that might not be Phil. It just looks like him. Weirdly."

Brian started to cry. "That's Phil," he insisted. "That's really Phil. Just like the scarecrows outside the cottage. Caleb and Jonathan. That's what the smiling man does. He makes scarecrows. He's going to make us all scarecrows!"

"No," said Coco, looking scared. "That's not it. That can't be it. Why would he do that?"

Ollie said nothing. She agreed with Brian. The scarecrow was Phil done in thread and yarn, the height, the backward cap . . . everything. His hands ended in two garden forks.

She put a hand, a little uncertain, on Brian's shaking shoulder. "I'm sure that we can find a way to fix it."

Brian's eyes were wet. *"Fix it?* That's my best buddy. Even if he is annoying sometimes. And he's a scarecrow. A *scarecrow.* Maybe he's dead. Maybe that's not him any-more—"

Ollie grabbed Brian's shoulders and spun him around so that he wasn't facing the scarecrow. "He's not dead," Ollie said firmly. "We're going to figure this out. We *are.* Brian, if we panic, we'll end up scarecrows too." She had no doubt it was true.

Brian drew a shuddering breath. "Okay," he said. "Okay." To the Phil scarecrow he said, "Don't worry, buddy. If you're in there, we're going to save you."

"We'll change him back, Brian," said Coco with what Ollie thought was impressive sincerity, seeing that Phil had humiliated her in front of the whole school. "I know we will."

"There has to be a way to fix it," Ollie said. "Like Narnia in winter—that got fixed. Or *Sleeping Beauty,* when the castle all woke up. That's what we have to do."

Brian wiped his eyes. "Okay," he said again, straighten-ing his shoulders. "But I'm only kissing Phil if I absolutely have to."

Ollie and Coco stared at him and then the three laughed. Their laughter was feeble, but it helped. Ollie glanced again at the cornfield and its crowd of scarecrows. Were they moving, just out of sight? Getting ready for the night?

"That's Jenna and Lily!" Coco whispered, pointing at two scarecrows just visible in the kitchen garden. The two scarecrows were holding hands, their mouths identical frightened Os.

"Let's try the house first," said Ollie after a long, grim look at the girls' frozen faces. "Like my watch said."

They went around the kitchen garden and passed behind the toolshed, whose splintery door hung crooked. They skirted the red barn. Everywhere scarecrows. In the garden, along the paths.

Ollie, Brian, and Coco recognized many of them. Others they didn't. Some of the scarecrows wore old-fashioned hats and dresses. Others wore jeans, carried backpacks.

Coco was shaking her head. "No," she said. "They can't all be . . . people."

Ollie and Brian didn't say anything. "Come on," said Ollie. "Let's try the house."

19

IN THE STRANGE shadow world, Linda Webster's fresh-painted farmhouse was faded, old, and ugly. Its door hung a little open, making Ollie think of spiders' webs.

If we were the flies.

But she marched forward anyway. Just as she got to the open door, with Brian and Coco too far back to hear, Ollie glanced down at her watch. UP, it said. Ollie looked up, but there was nothing there.

Despite herself, she whispered, "Mom? Is that you? Can you hear me?"

Silence. Only the rustling of corn.

Then the screen flickered. ALWAYS, it said.

Ollie closed her eyes, pressed the watch to her lips, felt herself shake. "I want to talk to you," she said, softer still.

Silence. UP, the watch said again.

Ollie glanced back into the farmyard. Had all the

scarecrows been facing the house before? Because all those faces—every single one of those scarecrow faces—was pointed toward the front door. "Guys," said Ollie. "Look. Have the scarecrows . . ."

Brian and Coco turned—and shuddered. All the scarecrows had their hands up. The light glinted dully on the tips of the rakes, the edges of scythes and trowels. "Yes," Brian whispered. "They definitely moved."

"Come inside," said Ollie, trying to sound as brave as she could. "Let's look around. We just have to hurry." She went into the house with her two friends at her heels.

The floorboards creaked. The wallpaper was coming off in streamers. A little thin daylight trickled in the dirty windows, but shadows seemed to lie thick in the corners. To their right lay a sitting room, with torn pink fabric on the walls. In front of them was a staircase leading up into the blackness of the second floor. To the left was the kitchen.

"Hello?" called Coco. "Is anyone here?"

No answer. Ollie looked at her watch. 45:16, said the countdown. UP.

Ollie headed into the kitchen. Coco and Brian followed. There was no sound but the squeaking floorboards. The kitchen was full of old-fashioned plates and cups and pots, all covered with a thick layer of dust. The woodstove was rusty, the wood beside it bone-dry.

"I think we should go upstairs," said Ollie. "My watch says UP."

Brian was already poking through the woodpile. "Hang on. There's kindling here," he said. "I'm going to make a fire, if I can find some matches."

"And let everyone know we're here?" Ollie snapped.

Brian shrugged. "The scarecrows know already," he pointed out. "If anyone else is out there, they probably know too. I'm cold. You're cold. Coco's got wet feet and she's probably really cold."

Coco's small face looked pale and pinched under Ollie's rainbow hat. "Just a bit cold," she said stubbornly.

"You'll be a lot warmer with dry socks," said Brian. "We'll make a fire and dry them. Tell your mom to buy you wool socks next time. Cotton's no good."

"If the chimney's blocked, you'll burn the house down," Ollie warned, but only halfheartedly. Brian was right. Coco was really pale; they didn't want her getting sick.

"Well," said Brian with a ghost of good cheer, "let's find out." He began to lay a fire. "I bet Coco'd kill for dry socks, let alone risk burning the house down."

"You do that," Ollie said. "I'm still going upstairs."

"I don't think we should split up," said Coco. "What if someone—what if a bad thing comes?"

"It's not dark yet," Ollie said.

"That's not the only bad thing!" cried Coco. "What about the ghost?"

"She wasn't *bad*," said Ollie. "Just dead."

Coco looked exasperated. "She was scary! I'm staying down here," she said just as Brian cried, "Matches!" He popped out of the pantry covered in cobwebs, waving a dusty old matchbox.

"Are you *sure* this is a good idea?" asked Coco. But she looked happier than she had in a while. Who could blame her? Even Ollie was cold and she was wearing more clothes and was used to being outside all the time.

"Yep!" said Brian. He began putting wood in the stove.

"Hope it works," said Coco eagerly.

Ollie unzipped her backpack and pulled out her unicorn lunch box. She broke off a piece of the pumpkin pie and put the rest on the table. "Here," said Ollie. "We should all eat something before it gets dark. Try not to burn the house down. I'm going upstairs."

Ollie marched off, chomping her portion of the slice of pie, leaving Brian and Coco going through her lunch box on the scarred kitchen table. A little fire had begun to sputter in the stove. Ollie wondered if she wasn't doing something really dumb, going off by herself.

The first bedroom was just to the right of the top of the staircase. The wallpaper had a pattern of cherries, which should have been cheerful except the paper was stained and the only light came from the gloomy outdoors. The bed had a moth-eaten red blanket. A vanity table with empty bottles. A bookcase. Ollie paused in the doorway, glancing behind her. Nothing. Just a hallway, with stairs at one end and the other end dark.

Ollie bit her lip. Each step she took made the floor creak. Ollie crept closer to the bookcase. A Bible. *A Book of Common Prayer. A Child's Guide to Virtue. Mrs. Beardsley's Domestic Sciences.*

Another floorboard creaked. It took her a moment to realize it wasn't her. She whirled. Steps. Coming from the darkness at the end of the hall. Soft, steady steps. Ollie froze.

A hand appeared on the doorframe. A thin, yellow-nailed hand.

Then a face popped around the edge of the doorframe. A gasp came strangling out of Ollie's throat. It was a woman. Or had been. Her skin was sunken in beneath the cheekbones, and when she smiled, her lips stretched too wide, the way a skull smiles. She stood in the doorway, blocking Ollie's escape.

"Who are you?" Ollie whispered. Her voice came out thin and scared.

A dry whisper murmured back, "My name is Beth Webster."

Ollie's spine was pressing up against the bookcase. "Beth Webster is dead."

The woman in the doorway said nothing. But her smile grew and grew, humorlessly, until it took up her entire lower face. Ollie had to bite back a scream. "I died in this room," whispered the woman. The rustle of her clothes sounded like dead leaves. "On the other side of the mist."

"How did you get to—this side?" Ollie managed to ask around her dry throat.

"Jonathan is here," Beth said. She clasped her hands together, long-fingered and bony. "The dead go where they will, and I wouldn't leave him. Wouldn't leave the farm when I was alive and won't leave him now. Even the smiling man can't make me. He'd like it, though. Oh yes he would."

"Why?" Ollie asked. Her lungs felt squeezed with fright.

"Because he doesn't have any power over the dead," said Beth. "And I'm not forgetting myself like Cathy did. Poor Cathy Webster, there's not much left of her now."

"Forgetting yourself?" asked Ollie. "Is Cathy forgetting herself? But—why is she here? Because her sons are?"

"Yes," said Beth. "Cathy wouldn't leave her children, not for anything. But that's what happens to ghosts. Their minds go, and then you are only memory, doing the same things over and over."

"Then why aren't you like that?" asked Ollie. She had begun to recover from her fright. Beth was scary, but she just stood in the doorway and *looked*.

"I wrote a book," said Beth thoughtfully. "I think that's

why. I put myself into it, all my days and nights and hopes and dreams. My whole life. I think my book is the reason I still remember. Although maybe it would have been easier to forget."

Maybe that's why the smiling man wanted Linda Webster to get rid of the book, Ollie thought. *To stop Beth from hanging around.* Ollie thought of the watch's instruction: UP. Maybe Beth Webster knew something important.

"Do you know how my friends and I can get home?" she asked. "Do you know how to turn the scarecrows back into people? Do you know how to beat the smiling man?"

The ghost laughed a long, shrill burst. "The smiling man is older than old," said Beth, still grinning. "You can't beat him. You might be happier in the corn with him. At least scarecrows feel nothing."

"Shut up!" snapped Ollie. "We aren't going to be scarecrows. I'm going home to my dad. How do we get home?"

"The cornfield is the doorway," said the ghost. "It's a maze, a corn maze. The scarecrows exist here and there. They are neither flesh nor spirit; they hold the door open for him. They are his servants in this world and his gatekeepers in the other." Big tears, as horrible as her laughter, ran down her bony nose. "And *I* am only a ghost, and my love is a scarecrow, and the servant of that horrible man." Her sad mouth seemed to droop down her face, as though the skin was rotten.

"How do we change the scarecrows back?" Ollie asked, torn between pity and horror.

"I do not know. 'Until the mist becomes rain,'" Jonathan told me once. But I don't know what that means. I am sorry," she said with a new note in her voice. "You have to go now."

That was when Ollie heard her watch beeping. Insistently. She realized how thick the shadows had grown. She looked down at her watch.

05:00.

Five minutes.

"I should have told you sooner," whispered Beth Webster. She was crying dusty, waterless tears. "I'm sorry, I'm sorry. But what was the use? You're never leaving this place. Nevernevernever . . ."

20

OLLIE HURRIED TO the window, heart thudding. The house was surrounded. The scarecrows' blind eyes stared up.

Ollie ran for the door, burst past the ghost, and then she was racing down the stairs. "Brian! Coco!" Behind her, the ghost screamed out a long wail of despair.

The kitchen smelled of burning. Ollie ran in, found herself coughing. The oven was billowing smoke, and Brian and Coco sat at the table, dazed. Ollie ran forward furiously to shake them by the shoulders. Brian stared up at her, red-eyed.

"This is why you don't make fires in strange stoves," Ollie growled. "They smoke and you *die*." Brian was getting clumsily to his feet, shaking his head, coughing. Coco, much smaller, was mostly unconscious. "Help me!" Ollie cried. She grabbed Coco's shoes and socks, still drying on the stove, and heaved them and her lunch box back into her backpack.

Brian, stumbling, propped Coco under his shoulder. They all staggered out of the kitchen. "It's almost dark," said Ollie as they went. "The scarecrows are outside."

"We'll have to hide in here, then," said Brian.

"No locks on the doors," said Ollie. "If there's a cellar, I didn't see it." She had an image of them cowering in a closet that didn't lock, while those slow, shuffling scarecrows beat the door down. Coco whimpered but didn't wake. "The barn!" Ollie cried. "It probably has a hayloft. We could pull up the ladder."

"Are you sure?" Brian asked.

"No," said Ollie. "But I think it's better than here. Our best chance." She looked at her watch. "Three minutes."

Brian unexpectedly slung Coco over his shoulders in what Ollie vaguely recalled was a fireman's carry.

"The Boy Scouts are no joke, are they?" she asked.

Brian grinned crookedly and then they ran for the front door. Outside it was the very edge of night, blue-black sky, clouds, no stars. The scarecrows clustered thick around the house, waiting. The light was almost gone. Ollie looked down at her watch. Forty-five seconds.

"We can't go out there!" Brian whispered, recoiling. "It's too late. They'll make us scarecrows too!"

"They won't," Ollie whispered back. "It's not night yet. Come on." She slipped out of the house and started across the yard. Brian followed more slowly, carrying Coco. The scarecrows stood perfectly still, snarling or smiling, their faces paper-bag white in the last of the daylight.

Ollie and Brian dodged around them, and then broke into a stumbling run, heading for the barn. Just as they passed the last of the scarecrows, Ollie's watch beeped and they were out of time.

Footsteps behind them. Ollie darted into the barn, praying. Brian was only a step behind her. Coco, waking up, saw what was behind them and shrieked.

Ollie spun to look. The scarecrows were shuffling toward the barn.

Brian shot into the barn on Ollie's heels and dropped Coco, none too gently, to the dusty wooden floor. He and Ollie heaved the barn door shut, looked at each other, and each took a grip on a handle. There was no lock.

They were left in pitch-darkness. Coco, with trembling hands, got her phone out and shone her light around. The hayloft was there. No ladder. Ollie felt the first creeping of despair. This wasn't a small space, not small enough. The scarecrows could get in. She could hear their shuffling steps just outside. She was holding on to the door handle for all she was worth.

"The ladder's in the hayloft," said Coco, coughing. She craned on her tiptoes. "I can see it!"

"A lot of good it will do us there," said Brian between gritted teeth. A steady pressure grew on the other side of the door, as if many hands had seized hold of the outside handles and were beginning to push.

"Wait!" cried Coco. "Wait, *wait*."

"Yeah," grunted Brian. "Tell the scarecrows to wait because that always works."

Coco ignored him.

"Shut up and hang on," said Ollie grimly to Brian. She had seen what Coco was doing and her heart beat fast with desperate hope. Coco ran barefoot for the barn walls, tripping on loose floorboards. The barn had a post-and-beam construction, so that the posts that supported the barn structure stuck out a bit from the wall itself. Coco threw off her backpack and wiped her sweaty hands on her jeans.

"Coco, anytime now!" screamed Ollie. From the other side of the door came scrapes and thuds. The veins were standing out in Brian's hands; he and Ollie had all their weight against the door, but they were both in danger of being yanked off their feet.

The door shook. Brian yelled. "I can't hold it!"

"We have to," said Ollie.

Coco let out a deep breath, grabbed the post, and began climbing. Ollie kept half an eye on her progress even as she felt splinters from the door handle work their way into her hands. Once Coco slipped and nearly fell, and Ollie seemed to feel the jolt in her own body. "Come on, Coco!" she shouted.

Now Coco was at the height of the hayloft, high enough

above the barn floor to break a leg if she fell. Now was the trickiest part, where she would have to let go of the post she'd climbed, reach out, and grab the lip of the hayloft. Coco hesitated. The door shook. "Coco!" Brian yelled.

Coco let go of the post, caught the edge of the hayloft, and swung a moment in space, one-handed. Ollie saw the hand slipping; her heart seemed to leap into her mouth. But then Coco's other hand shot out and she pulled herself up. From as far as the barn door, Ollie could hear the whine of her breathing, almost a sob. But then Coco heaved herself to her feet and the next moment the heavy hayloft ladder slid down and landed *thump* on the floor.

"Come on, guys!" Coco yelled from above.

"If we can brace the door with something," panted Ollie, "it might give us time to get up to the hayloft, pull the ladder up after us."

"What if they can climb?" said Coco from above. "Or jump?" She was still breathing hard.

"They can't," said Ollie, hoping that she was right. "They have garden tools for hands!"

"There!" cried Coco. She was shining her phone light around the barn floor. It lit up a pile of rusty shovels.

Brian and Ollie looked at each other. "Can you hold the doors?" Ollie asked him.

"For about five seconds," Brian grunted. He took a new grip on the door and gritted his teeth.

"Now!" cried Ollie. She let go of the handle, ran to the pile of tools, and grabbed a shovel. Brian's arms were trembling; the door had already begun to give.

"Ollie!" he screamed just as she sprinted back and jammed the old wooden shovel handle sideways between the door handles.

Brian let go. It shook, but held. "Will it last?" asked Brian, panting.

"Probably not," said Ollie grimly. "But it might last long enough."

It was witch-soul dark in the barn, except for the stabbing beam of Coco's phone light.

"Come on!" Coco cried. She pointed her phone at the ladder. The shovel handle was already splintering.

"Go on, Ollie," said Brian, shoving her toward the ladder. When she hung back, he said, *Go on.* The ghost of a smile. "Chivalry, remember?"

Ollie met his eyes and without a word began climbing the hayloft ladder. No time to think of the height, not even time to be scared.

Coco's light jerked up from the ladder to the door. Ollie risked a glance back. She was more than halfway to the loft. The old shovel handle was bending. With a *crack*, it gave. Now the door was sliding open. A soft painted-on face thrust itself into the gap.

Ollie made it into the hayloft just as the first scarecrows

shuffled into the barn. Brian, right behind her, was still on the ladder.

"Hurry, Brian!" Coco cried. "Hurry!"

I hope they can't jump, Ollie thought. *I hope they can't climb.* The scarecrows had surrounded the ladder, shaking it from side to side. Brian made a desperate grab for the lip of the hayloft just as the old ladder went tumbling sideways and crashed down onto the barn floor.

"Brian!" Ollie yelled. She and Coco hurled themselves forward at the same moment and grabbed his hands. The ladder lay on the barn floor, and Brian was dangling, feet over the splintered wood, above the grinning scarecrows. They made a whispering sound like straw rustling as they reached up their garden-rake hands.

Brian was heavy. His feet swung and kicked in midair. Ollie and Coco pulled together, pulled as hard as they could. Their sweaty hands slipped and slid. For a terrible moment, Ollie thought Brian's hand would slip right out of hers, that he would fall to the barn floor, just like the ladder, and be snatched by scarecrows.

But Brian, gasping, got a foot up. Then another. A last, panicked tug and they were all in a trembling heap in the hayloft, safe for the moment but with no way to get down.

Could the scarecrows get up? That was the question.

The scarecrows glared at them. But Ollie had been right. They couldn't climb with their garden-tool hands.

One of them tried to pick up the ladder. But Brian and Ollie and Coco kicked it off when they tried to lean the ladder against the hayloft. This time, when the ladder fell to the floor, it broke into two pieces and was unusable.

"We're safe," whispered Coco. "We're safe." Her phone light flickered over the scarecrow faces.

"Maybe safe," whispered Ollie. For more and more scarecrows were pouring into the barn. Among them were several they recognized. There was Denise Carter, and then Elodie Finnegan. Jim Johnson. Their hands were garden tools. All of them button eyed, with lips of string.

Ollie swallowed. "Let's see if they can talk," she said. "Maybe they can tell us something useful."

"How can they talk?" Coco asked.

"Dunno. How can they walk? Hey!" Ollie shouted, before she could lose her nerve. "Hey! Can you talk?"

A sound from the scarecrows like the rattling of straw. Then Phil's face looked up at them. Brian let out a pained breath. A hole in Phil's straw mouth opened. A voice spoke like the wind in the wheat in summer. "Come down," breathed Phil. "Come down and join us. It's nice. You'll like it. You live forever and you'll never be sad again."

Phil the idiot, Ollie had always thought. The guy who stuck girls' hair to the back of their seats with gum. But Brian was staring at his friend, his face blank with horror.

She reached out to take Brian's hand; on the other side, she saw Coco doing the same thing.

"Ask him," whispered Ollie. "Ask him if he remembers anything."

Brian licked his lips. "Hey, Phil . . ." Gone was the hockey swagger, his voice a cracked whisper, not much better than the sound of a scarecrow. "What happened, man?"

"Come down," returned the scarecrow.

"*No,*" said Brian violently. "Don't you remember? I'm Brian. Brian. We caught tadpoles in the creek when we were little. Your mom makes the best blueberry pie in the world. You were mad when I made the hockey team and you didn't, but you never said one word to me except 'way to go'—"

Suddenly Phil's face moved more like a real face, just visible in the light of Coco's phone.

"Brian?" whispered the scarecrow, in a different voice. "Brian, where are we?"

Brian's hand was trembling in Ollie's, but his voice was steady when he said, "I have no idea. How'd you get this way, huh? Can you tell me that?"

"He smiled at us," breathed the scarecrow. "I only remember the smile . . ." Then the scarecrow's limbs jerked in a way that wasn't at all human. "Maze," he whispered. "In the maze." The brief humanity was gone from his face, fast as it had come. He was only a scarecrow, standing stiff in the straw. They stood in massed ranks, not looking up now, just standing, empty as dolls. Waiting.

Brian bowed his head. He was still shaking. Coco's phone reflected a little light into their faces, making them look like specters in the darkness of that haunted world. They were all still holding hands. "At least Phil is still in there, somewhere," said Coco. "He's not—gone. He remembered you. I'm sure he did."

Brian didn't answer.

They didn't say anything for a while.

"We ought to keep a watch," said Ollie, rousing herself.

"If they could climb, they would be doing it already," said Coco.

"Still," said Ollie.

After another pause, she said, "I met Beth Webster's ghost in the front bedroom."

Brian and Coco both swung around to look at her. "She said that the smiling man was in the center of the maze," continued Ollie. "That the maze is his doorway between worlds and that the scarecrows hold it open somehow. After what Phil said—I think that's where we have to go. Into the maze."

"It could be a trap," Coco pointed out. She had begun to shiver as hard as Brian, as the shock from terror and climbing wore off. Ollie saw that her hands were full of splinters and bloodied. She realized that neither Brian nor Coco could take any more thinking or speculation that night. "We should get some sleep," Ollie said firmly. "And decide in the morning. Brian, where's that first-aid kit? Coco's hurt herself. And I definitely have splinters and you probably do too."

"It doesn't matter," Brian said. "It doesn't matter if your hands have splinters when you have trowels for hands!" He giggled hysterically.

Ollie whacked him in the arm. "Stop that right now," she said. "That's not helping. First-aid kit. Then Coco's going to share some trail mix—no, wait, your backpack's still down there, isn't it, Coco? Well, I'll share some granola, then, and we're all going to drink some water and take turns getting some sleep. 'Kay?"

"Okay, Ollie," Brian said, his voice thin and tired now.

He and Ollie took turns picking the big ugly splinters out of Coco's hands. Coco didn't make a sound. After a liberal application of alcohol and Snoopy Band-Aids, Coco said, "Thanks, guys."

"Hey," said Ollie, "you kind of saved our lives back there."

Coco looked pleased. "I did, didn't I?" she said.

They de-splintered Brian, then Ollie. They shared the granola, and Ollie again blessed her dad's overpacking. "Peanut butter and jelly for skiing," he used to say. "Ham and cheese for hiking."

Ollie tried to let that memory warm her as the three took off their shoes and piled up their coats and backpacks to make something to sleep on. "I'll keep watch for a bit. I want to do some thinking, anyway," said Ollie. "Get some sleep, guys."

Brian and Coco settled themselves among the coats. Ollie wished she had grabbed the dusty blanket from the bedroom upstairs. Eventually the others fell asleep. But Ollie did not. She sat peering over the edge of the loft for a long time. She thought about ghosts and scarecrows, of a world hidden under the real one. Of a person called the smiling man.

Of bargains.

Until at last, Ollie, unable to keep her eyes open, woke Brian and tried to get some sleep herself.

21

WHEN COCO WOKE her up, it was morning. Ollie glanced down at the space beneath them first. The scarecrows were still there, but the life was gone from them. They were only a mass of straw dolls. Ollie glanced at her watch. The countdown had resumed: 06:13:21.

MAZE.

Brian sat up, groaning. "Are they gone?" he asked.

"No," said Ollie. "They're down there." They all peered over the edge and shuddered.

"How are we supposed to get down?" Coco asked. For of course the ladder was broken.

"We could jump down," said Brian unenthusiastically. "Maybe the scarecrows would break our fall?"

"Or they wouldn't and we'd break our ankles," said Coco.

"We can't just sit up here forever," said Ollie.

"Fine," said Brian shortly. "You jump first."

"Hush. Hear that?" Coco said.

Ollie and Brian fell silent. Rub. Creak. It sounded like slow feet right overhead. They all froze.

Then suddenly Ollie laughed. She stood up. "No scarecrows this time," she said. "A tree branch rubbing the roof. And that means a tree, which means a way down. The roof tiles are all rotten." She began scraping at the roof from the inside. Wormy wood rained down around her. "Come on, help me."

Together they made a hole big enough to boost Coco's head through. "A tree branch!" cried Coco. "Ollie, you were right. Here—" She grabbed something they couldn't see and struggled out, kicking. "It's fine," said Coco, muffled overhead. "You just have to climb. Carefully."

"How is she the clumsiest person ever on the ground, yet a squirrel when she's climbing?" muttered Ollie.

Brian grinned. "You're kind of grumpy most of the time, but when things get bad, you're the bravest. People can surprise you, Ollie-pop." Without another word, he turned away and began making the hole in the roof bigger.

Ollie found herself smiling. "Yeah, sometimes even hockey stars read books," she said.

"Sometimes," said Brian, and smiled back. "You next."

Ollie hoisted her backpack and let him push her out

the hole in the roof. She found herself high above the world, looking out at the huge, rustling field of corn. There seemed to be a dark lump in the center of the field, but she couldn't tell what it was.

Ollie waited to be scared sick of the height. But she wasn't.

Coco had used the branch rubbing the barn roof like a bridge. Now she was watching anxiously from the fork of the big old oak tree. "Come on, Ollie!" she called.

Behind her, Brian said, "Come on, Ollie. It's not that high."

And Olivia Adler, without hesitation, crawled across the branch and began climbing down the tree. In a few minutes, they were all on the ground, flushed with success.

———

The cornstalks hissed all together. They were taller than Brian's head. Scarecrows stood in the corn; the trio caught glimpses of bright shirts and checked shirts. None of them really wanted to go into the field.

"Well," said Ollie, "either we wait for the scarecrows to come back tonight and every night until they get us or we starve. Or we go into the corn."

"We can't leave without the others," said Brian. "Once you leave Narnia, you can't get back in the same way."

Ollie nodded. "If anyone is going to save them, it has to be us." She raised her watch. MAZE, it said. "The answer has to be in there."

"Fine," said Coco, looking unhappily at the corn. "Fine!"

They were like swimmers about to jump into icy water and no one wanted to go first.

"Let's go," said Ollie. She reached out her hands. Brian and Coco took them.

The three stepped into the corn. The path was narrow and they switched to single file. Ollie went first, then Coco, then Brian. Their feet squelched in the mud. Such big stalks—the corn looked like it could swallow the gray sky, much less three wandering kids.

They were walking down a row. Ollie could barely hear her own footsteps, couldn't hear Brian's and Coco's. The corn rustled too loudly, dead stalks rubbing together.

The row ended. Ollie looked up at a huge wall of corn. They could turn left or right. "Okay," said Ollie. "It's definitely a corn maze. We have to get to the center. Any ideas?"

Ollie had loved corn mazes when she was small. Left then right, squealing in fake terror, mud flying as she ran, and then finally figuring it out, getting to the center, laughing, her father picking her up, saying, "Way to go, Ollie-pop. No maze can stop you." But this was different. This was cold and huge and scary.

"Guys?" said Ollie, turning.

Coco and Brian were gone.

The winds whispered in the cornstalks. "Guys?"

Silence.

Ollie began to backtrack. "Coco?" she called. "Brian?" Ollie could see only one set of footsteps, only hers, the print of her rain boots. Where had they gone? For that matter, where was the way they'd come in? For now, another wall of corn rose right in front of her, and she couldn't see the house, or the barn. How was that possible? She'd—*they'd*—walked straight in, not turning. But now there were walls on two sides and Coco and Brian weren't there.

Ollie felt close to panic. She spun, headed the other direction, deeper into the corn. *Shush*, went the stalks all around. Ollie thought she saw a dark shape up ahead.

She ran, calling, "Brian!" But it was only a scarecrow with a yellow backpack, staked upright, looking out over the field with sightless eyes. There was no other sound but the hissing corn and the whine of Ollie's own breathing.

What if something had taken the others—just sneaked up through the corn and dragged them away? Something worse than the scarecrows?

The smiling man? Maybe he was watching her even now.

"Coco?" Ollie called again. "Brian?"

Someone yelled. "Ollie! Ollie!"

Ollie spun. "Coco?"

"Ollie!" the voice called again. Ollie began to run, calling her friends' names.

She came to the place where the path split. Left or right? Rustling in the corn . . . Was that something coming up behind her?

Ollie chose a direction at random—left—and took off running. Her backpack thumped her back. "Brian! Coco!" The corn rattled. The sky blurred. Ollie passed a scarecrow, then another. Furiously, she kicked the last one down so that it lay still in the mud, looking up at the sky with its empty smiling face. Ollie was in a panic by then, alone, sobbing for air, stuck in the maze. She would never get out and all around her were the scarecrows with their snatching rake hands just waiting for the night to grab her and put her on a stake and make her a scarecrow forever.

Then Ollie put her foot in a hole, tripped, and came down hard. She could taste the salt of her tears. She lay a moment in the icy mud, crying. She was lost in a monster's stupid corn maze and she was all alone. She wasn't going to get out. Not before dark. What would her dad do when she never came back?

There was a sound coming from underneath her, a sound different from the sound of the wind in the corn.

It took Ollie a moment to understand. One arm was stuck beneath her, the arm that wore her mother's watch.

The watch was beeping, softly and steadily. Like a heartbeat. Like something calm. *Don't panic,* Ollie's mom had always told her. *That's the first rule of survival. Never panic.* Ollie took a deep breath. That was probably what the smiling man wanted, for her to wear herself out running and being scared. Ollie sat up and then she stood. Her jeans were covered in cold, sticky mud. "I'm not scared," Ollie said. "I'm not. I'm going to find the center. I'm getting out of here. We all are."

She looked at her watch. The text readout was gone. In its place was a digital compass.

"Mom?" Ollie whispered. "Mom, if you're here, please..."

No answer. *Please what,* Ollie thought, mad at herself. *Please answer? Please drift out of the corn, a ghost?*

Please don't be dead?

The watch buzzed softly against Ollie's wrist. The readout showed a compass needle, but instead of the normal NSEW directions, there were only two:

There was an *I* where north should be. There was an *O* where south should be.

Ollie thought a minute and then she understood. IN the maze or OUT. Maybe OUT was safer. No scarecrows. But IN . . . IN was finding Brian and Coco. IN was maybe saving everyone. IN was being brave. Like her mom had been brave. Always, always. Her mom was the bravest person Ollie had ever met. Ollie could be brave. Her mom was helping her. She was.

Ollie swung around until IN lined up with the path. "Show me," she whispered.

22

OLLIE WALKED THROUGH the corn for hours. There were a lot of scarecrows, and more and more seemed to appear as she went on. Though she never saw their heads move, they always watched her come and they always watched her go.

Sometimes she would call for Brian or Coco. No one answered. Ollie stopped once to drink from her water bottle. It was half-empty. She got cold, kept moving, wishing for pizza. It was definitely afternoon. But no countdown had appeared on her watch, just the directions leading her into the maze, IN and steadily IN.

The sun had begun to fall toward the horizon in a low autumn arc when she heard a new sound in the corn, like something big was moving through it. Then a long slow breath.

Ollie froze. It sounded like a huge dog breathing. Definitely not the sound of a scarecrow. The steps were getting closer. Ollie crept between two stalks of corn and hid.

A creature came snuffling down the long line of the maze.

Ollie didn't realize she was biting her lip until she tasted blood. It was a dog—sort of. It had a coat the color of mushrooms, a snout like a hound, paws like a cat, and eyes of a perfect egg white. Its sides went in and out, and its breathing was louder than the cornstalks. It made Ollie think of the minotaur in the labyrinth.

The beast came closer, growling low in its chest. It paused. Sniffed the air. Sniffed again. Its ears swiveled towards Ollie, and then it peered between the cornstalks and saw her.

She stared into eyes white as two cooked eggs and she could barely breathe.

The beast didn't move. But it growled again. "Come out, little girl. Come out." Talking. Like a person. The ege of a fang just showed beheath its lip.

Ollie tried to think. Those eyes. That voice. Were they—were they familiar? She'd seen egg-white eyes before. Seen them pressed up against a bus window. Watching her. Just like they were doing now.

At night they'll come for the rest of you.

She swallowed. And then she spoke, squeaking. "Are you—are you the bus driver?"

The beast didn't answer directly. But it's mouth dropped open, panting. She saw the red tongue, the red lips.

"Come out," the beast whispered again, and this time reached out a stealthy, clawed foot.

Ollie jumped back, and then on a surge of fear and desperation, wrenched around and dug into her backpack. She scrabbled in her lunch box and on a burst of courage, thrust her way out of the corn, held out two of her dad's peanut butter cookies and said, "Don't you dare touch me. I gave you food once before. Do you want some more?"

She hoped she was right. She prayed she was right. Her hand holding the cookies shook.

The beast had stepped back. It shut its mouth and eyed her. Its tongue flicked out, as though tasting the air. He licked his chops. His tongue darted toward the cookies.

Ollie stepped back. "No," she said. "You have to trade me for it. Remember?"

Silence. Then a hoarse, deep voice crept out between the beast's teeth. "What trade, little girl?"

If her classmates were scarecrows, Ollie thought a little hysterically, then it wasn't too strange that their bus driver was a giant wolf-creature.

Ollie said, "Where are my friends?"

"Lost," said the wolf. "Lost until dark, and then— scarecrows."

Ollie broke off a piece of cookie and fed it to him. He licked it up with surprising delicacy.

"Do you know where they are?"

"Yes."

She fed him another piece, thinking. Her watch would get her to the center of the maze. But Brian and Coco . . .

Ollie closed her fist on the remains of her cookies. She said, "I'll give you the rest—I'll give you all the food I have—if you go find my two friends, Brian and Coco, and bring them to the center of the maze. Before dark. If," Ollie added hastily, "you don't hurt them on the way."

"It won't help," breathed the creature. "Even if you all get to the center. What he has, he holds."

"We'll see," said Ollie, and held out her cookies.

The creature snapped them up, then practically inhaled the rest of her food. Ollie, a little forlornly, put her empty lunch box back in her backpack, hoping she'd done the right thing. The beast licked his chops. "He doesn't feed me good things," he said. "Only souls, sometimes. The used-up ones, dry as dead corn."

Without another word, the creature turned and stalked away.

———————

It was almost dark when the corn finally ended. Ollie found herself at the edge of an open space.

The middle of the maze.

The open space was full of scarecrows. They stood in a ragged ring, arms stretched out. Their big garden-tool hands seemed to reach for her. Many of them she recognized: her classmates, horribly changed. She saw the two tall scarecrows in black suits from those moments in Cathy's house. Caleb and Jonathan. Perhaps she was imagining it, but there almost seemed to be a look of pleading on their faces. On *all* those blank, sewn-on faces.

In the very center of the maze was a platform, like a farmer might use to keep an eye on the corn. Ollie couldn't see the top of it. A ladder led up to a hole in the center.

The scarecrows glared, sightless yet somehow seeing. Ollie thought she saw two women, the ghosts of Beth and Cathy, hiding among the scarecrows, watching. *A living girl.* The whisper seemed to rise from the corn itself. *A living girl, here.* Ollie took a deep breath and walked past the scarecrows. She walked all the way to the ladder that led to the center of the tall platform.

She began to climb.

Halfway up, Ollie looked back. All the scarecrows were watching her. Ollie's fingers tightened convulsively on the ladder rungs. Then she called down, "I am going to go home, and I am going to save you all."

Then she climbed up to the top.

———

Ollie didn't know what sort of thing she was expecting on a platform in the middle of a haunted corn maze. Horrors for sure, though she was almost too exhausted to be frightened. It was going to be dark very soon. An ugly reddish light bathed the scene.

"My," said a gentle voice, "all this way. Right to the center. And before dark. I'm impressed."

Ollie peered into the shadows gathering on the platform—and could hardly believe her eyes.

"*You!*" she gasped.

"Who did you expect?" asked Seth. His pale hair caught the last of the light. His eyes were as deep and his smile was as lovely as they had been at Misty Valley Farm. Behemoth the cat sat at his side, watching lamp-eyed in the almost dark.

"You're the smiling man," said Ollie slowly. She could barely believe it. "I thought—" She'd imagined a skull smile, a pumpkin-head smile. A scarecrow smile.

She'd not imagined a kind smile, the sort that would make a scared kid not be scared anymore.

"I am," said Seth. He was wearing his jeans, his flannel shirt, just like he was about to go milk cows. But there were no cows. Instead he was sitting on a platform at dusk with a hundred scarecrows at his feet. The cat twined around him, never taking its eyes off Ollie. "Your cat?" she whispered.

Seth smiled. "My servant. Cats are convenient. They go between worlds, their nature unchanged. The only creature that can. How do you think I kept track of you?"

Ollie remembered Coco thinking she'd seen an animal,

remembered Brian wondering if he'd imagined a creature's footsteps.

"The bus driver?" she asked, voice flat to stop it from shaking. His ordinary smiling face frightened her more than any number of ghosts.

"My hound," said Seth, and shrugged dismissively. "I sent him to bring you to me; folk can wander this maze until they die. It is bigger than it seems. Rather surprising you avoided him and came to the center on your own. Shame about your poor friends."

"You made that deal with Jonathan. A hundred years ago. More."

"I did," said Seth.

"Why?"

"Why not?"

"Why scarecrows then?"

He shrugged. "No one notices them in the sunlit world. They have hands; they are useful. They can be my eyes and my ears, and since they are neither flesh nor spirit, they can be my doorway." He grinned. "Also they are frightening, and I do love that."

"Ms. Webster knew who you were," Ollie pursued doggedly, trying not to hear the sound of scarecrows moving. "She was scared of you."

"Scared of *me*?" said Seth. He laughed, not kindly. "She was more afraid of the future. Her farm was about to go under. She was going to go to prison for fraud. All her pretty dreams sold in bankruptcy court, and all her sunlit life in nature cut short by bars. *I'll do anything,* she said.

I told her what she had to do if I was to save her farm for her, save her freedom for her. How she wept when I told her. But she paid the price. Mostly. She neglected to get rid of the book."

"We were the price," said Ollie. "The sixth grade." The day was nearly done.

"Of course. Although I did wonder if there would be someone clever enough to avoid the scarecrows. I even had my hound warn you. I wanted to know if there were any clever children. I thought you might be the one." He bowed, and the movement looked old-fashioned but strangely natural, despite his flannel shirt and jeans. "Although, little thief, I suppose Beth's book helped." His face showed a flash of malice. *He really wanted that book destroyed,* Ollie thought.

"I don't want congratulations," Ollie snapped. "I just want to go home."

"Of course," said Seth, surprising her. "You have made it to the center of the maze. Don't you want your reward?"

"Sure," said Ollie. "Send us home. All of us."

Seth smiled at her, a charming, boyish smile. Then his grin stretched and stretched again, wide as the cat in *Alice's Adventures in Wonderland*, so wide it literally stretched from ear to ear. Like dead Beth Webster.

Ollie screamed at him, screamed with a mix of terror and rage. "Don't you dare try to scare me! Don't you *dare!*"

Seth stepped back, laughing. "Lighten up! Why not, when it's fun? I've been scaring you for days. I'm not tired of it yet." He sobered. "See, girl, you say you want to get home. I know you do. But it's not the thing you want most in all the world. I know it. Tell me what you want most, Olivia Adler. I'm not in the business of granting second-rate wishes."

Before Ollie could answer, two things happened. Ollie's watch chimed. It was night. And from below the platform came the sound of two people shouting.

Ollie's breath seemed to fail in her throat. She looked over the platform edge just in time to see the huge dog that had been the bus driver herd Brian and Coco into the center of the maze, snapping and growling. The scarecrows clicked their garden-tool hands together. Like they were applauding. And then they seized Brian and Coco and held them tight.

"Let them go!" Ollie cried. How dumb was she, trusting the beast who'd been a bus driver just because he liked her dad's cooking?

Seth smiled at her sweetly this time, not with a skull grin like before. "Gladly," he said. "But is *that* really what you want most, clever girl? Decisions, decisions, Miss Adler. Do you want to go home safely with your little friends? Or do you want—?" He trailed off, head cocked, as though listening.

"I—" Ollie began, but then words failed her. A voice called from the corn. A voice she had known she would never hear in her whole life again.

"Olivia!" it called. "Olivia, where are you?"

Ollie froze. Brian and Coco were thrashing in the scarecrows' grip, but Ollie stopped seeing them. She couldn't see anything at all. She could only listen, listen for all she was worth. "*Mom!*" she cried. She spun toward the edge of the platform.

"Not so fast," came Seth's voice, sharp now from behind her. Ollie whipped back towards him, panting. "You've seen I have the goods. Now let's bargain, Olivia Adler. What will you give to have your mother back?"

Below her, both Brian and Coco were shouting her name. But she ignored them, straining to hear that other, beloved voice. "Sweetheart, please. It's so dark." Her mother. Her mother *right there*.

For a moment, Ollie forgot Brian and Coco, even forgot her father waiting for her somewhere beyond this nightmare. She just wanted her mom. *The smiling man brought Caleb back. Seth brought Caleb back.* He could do it. "What do you want?" she asked.

"For you, brave girl?" Seth said gently. "Not much. Not much at all. I'll let you go, you and your mother. You can even take your two friends with you. Four lives. Not bad, hm? But you can't have the rest. Mustn't be greedy. Leave the rest, and you drop the book in the river. I'm tired of

Beth Webster's ghost. And one day, a long time from now, when I knock on your door, you have to let me in. That's what I call a good deal." His eyes were earnest, kind.

Wild thoughts whirled through Ollie's brain. Brian. Coco. They could all escape together. She would come back from this nightmarish place holding her mother's hand.

Beth Webster's book lay heavy in her pocket. She thought of Caleb and Jonathan. *A drowned man breathed back to life would look like him.* Ollie swallowed hard. Then she turned back to the smiling man. "Okay," she said shakily. "Fine. Say I say yes. How do the four of us get home?"

He smiled. "The maze is the door. One of the exits will take you back into your own world. But only I know which. Make a deal and I'll show you the way. Is it a deal, Olivia Adler?" He put out his hand.

"Olivia, Olivia!" called her mother's voice.

Ollie didn't take the hand. "I don't want Brian and Coco," she said. "They're annoying. I want Jenna and Lily. But they're scarecrows. How do I take them with me? You promised me four lives."

Seth shrugged again. "Mist for capturing. Water for freeing. Lethe Creek runs through my world and yours. Let the scarecrows touch the water and they'll be as they were. Now shake."

Until the mist becomes rain, Ollie thought.

She was gripping the watch on her wrist, white-knuckled. Tears still ran freely down her face, but she managed a smile. "No thanks," she said. Seth stilled. The whole field seemed to hold its breath. "But now I know how to get out of here," Ollie added. "So thanks for that."

The cat yowled. "*Olivia!*" screamed her mother's voice, loving, desperate. It sounded like she was directly below her.

Ollie was clasping on her watch on her wrist so hard, the metal bit into her palm.

"That's not my mother," Ollie said to Seth. She held up her wrist with the watch. "My mother is already with me. Helping. Maybe she's a little easier to hear in this weird ghost world of yours. But I'm pretty sure she never left me, not at all, just like Cathy Webster never left her kids. So *you* are a liar and a fraud and we are going home!" She was sobbing as she spoke.

"Olivia!" cried her mom's voice once more, faint now.

"Well," said Seth, "that's a shame. Because, of course, if you don't make a deal to get out, you aren't getting out at all. You're already part of a bargain, you know. If you won't make a new one, well then, you'll be my servant too." Below, Ollie could hear creaking as the first of the scarecrows began coming up the ladder. "You will stand in the rain by day and walk my world at night. Keep the maze open and do my bidding."

"No," said Ollie. "Absolutely not."

Until the mist becomes rain. Well, Ollie wasn't about to conjure rain from the sky, so she did the only thing she could think of, which was pull her water bottle from its side pouch and fling a scattering of drops at the first scarecrow

204

coming up the ladder. The scarecrow screamed—a human scream. The cat hissed and jumped at Ollie, clawing at her face. Ollie threw it off and then Seth was there, tall and terrible, his mouth a great starving maw. But he *still* wasn't attacking her, Ollie realized, just trying to scare her.

In a voice still thick with tears, Ollie said, "*I* haven't made a bargain with you. If you made a deal with Ms. Webster, then it was a cheat, a fraud. She gave what she couldn't give: us. And I'm taking us back."

Seth's mouth closed, and Ollie knew she was right. He was a cold, tricky thing, but there were rules, and he'd broken one, taken what someone didn't have the right to give. "I can only *give* you power over me," said Ollie, more and more sure. "You can't take it. You said you'd give me water. Well, I have that too."

Seth looked less human now. His grin still took up half his face, but the eyes above were malevolent. "Little fool," he said. "I am older than you. I am stronger than you . . ."

"So?" said Ollie. "If you could have made me a scarecrow, you would have done it by now. But we hid in small spaces at night, and the scarecrows couldn't get to us, and now I am making no bargain with you. Not even for the deepest wish of my heart. So you can't do anything to me."

She splashed water on the next climbing scarecrow. Another human scream.

"They are the door," said Seth, speaking fast. He

205

definitely looked afraid now. "What will you do when they are all human? The door will close."

But Ollie smiled right back at Seth. "Do you know what else I'm pretty sure exists in both worlds? A book called *Small Spaces*. 'Cause it was bound and printed in Boston and it would be really weird if they'd only printed one copy. I have my copy right here. I guess you forget about that sort of thing when you're a super-old corn-maze monster."

They stared each other down. Seth spoke first. "Will you bet your life on it?" he whispered.

Ollie's mouth was bone-dry. "Yes," she said.

Seth bowed suddenly. "Check and mate to you," he said. "Clever girl."

Ollie, wary, said nothing.

In Seth's eyes was almost a look of wonder. "I will be back," he said. He didn't say it like a promise, but a fact. "Nevertheless, I thank you. I do not lose very often." He added, with a quirk of his mouth, "There is something you will want of me. One day."

"There will be things I want," said Olivia Adler, "but never of you."

"Call my hound by his name," said Seth, "and he will come." And then the smiling man smiled at her one more time. And bowed again, courtly. And disappeared.

23

BRIAN AND COCO sprinted up to her when she touched
the ground, and she found herself locked in a breathless
three-way hug, full of questions. "Ollie, what happened?"
asked Coco. "The scarecrows just let us go, and then the
two that were climbing the ladder fell back down again
and turned to dust."

"We won, I think," said Ollie. "The smiling man is
gone." She was so tired.

Loud, panting breaths came up out of the dark. Coco
and Brian shrank back. The driver, the hound, lifted his
great gray head and sniffed the three of them over. "It's
okay," said Ollie to Brian and Coco. "He helped me. I asked
him to bring you to the center of the maze. I was afraid
you were lost."

Brian scowled at the hound. "He scared me half to

death," he said. Coco was already reaching out to rub the hound's ears.

To the hound, Ollie said, "The smiling man said to call you and you'd come. But what's your name?"

"I have none," said the hoarse, panting voice. Brian and Coco both jumped again. "That's his trick too."

"Then let's be traditional and call you Cerberus, even though you don't have three heads," said Ollie. The beast shook himself and looked pleased. "Thanks," she added.

The bony ghosts of Beth and Cathy Webster stood beside two tall scarecrows dressed in old-fashioned black.

To Beth, Ollie said, "Thanks for writing your book. I'm pretty sure it saved our lives."

Beth looked pleased. "I hope you will keep it." She sighed and looked up. From between the clouds overhead gleamed a single star. "I am going on."

"Not alone, I hope," said Ollie.

Beth took the hand of the taller of the scarecrows and smiled at him. For a second it seemed the scarecrow was smiling back. "No, not alone."

The scarecrows fell to dust; the ghosts vanished.

———

The last drops of water were sprinkled on the last people. Ollie heard Mr. Easton sputtering, "What on *earth*?" as he heard Coco's soothing and creative explanation.

She looked down at her watch, swung the compass around until the needle pointed to O. "Let's go home," she said. "No one get lost, okay?"

It took them until dawn to get out of the corn maze, which twisted in on itself, again and again, like the minotaur's labyrinth. They *would* have been lost without Ollie's watch.

"I don't understand," said Mr. Easton over and over. "I don't understand." But he walked beside Ollie for a while and then went back with Brian to make sure no one was lost in the darkness and twisting stalks. The kids didn't talk much. They just walked, hanging on to each other, dull with shock.

For most of the way, Seth's hound went with them, breathing deep breaths like the rushing of the sea in the darkness.

Just at sunrise, they saw a gap where the corn ended.

24

THE SIXTH GRADE of Ben Withers Middle School came out of the corn maze together, and Brian, Ollie, and Coco were holding hands as they did. They were even laughing; who cared if they were dirty? They were alive. The sky was a thin living blue. The air smelled like ordinary fall: crisp leaves and smoke. There were no scarecrows. The mud and cold and fear of the past days was like a bad dream.

At the edge of the cornfield, the hound stopped. Ollie turned to look at him. "Call me by my name," he whispered into her ear, "if you need." And then he bounded joyfully back into the shadows between the corn, the shadows that, Ollie suspected, always clung to the edge of the world.

Then the kids stepped out of the corn maze and stopped.

"We're back where we started," said Brian.

They were. They had popped out of the cornfield

right next to the bus. The bus looked just as it had on the day they rode to Misty Valley Farm, except now it stood abandoned in the middle of the road.

A very serious crowd stood around the bus. A tow truck, three police cars. Regular cars were lined up on both sides of the road, with crowds of people dressed to tramp through the woods. A search party. Parents. All their parents. Some of them had obviously been crying. Ms. Webster was there, weeping hysterically. Her voice came to Ollie's ears as she stepped out of the corn. "The scare-crows," she was saying. "The scarecrows—and he smiled at me. I couldn't say no, d'ye hear me? I couldn't say no!"

I said no, said Ollie. *And I bet I wanted my mom more than you wanted your old farm, even if you were going to jail.*

Heads turned, as thirty kids broke at once from a gap in the corn. Some people screamed with happiness and shock. But Ollie only had eyes for one of them. "Dad!" Ollie hollered. *"Dad!"*

Her father whipped around. "Ollie? *Ollie!*" There was no color in his face, not even a bit, and there were marks like blue thumbprints under his eyes.

Her father sent Officer Perkins sprawling when he sprinted toward her. Parents on all sides were running toward their kids, shouting questions, exclaiming, crying. Ollie found that she was running too, half blinded by tears. All around her, the sixth grade surged forward.

"Mom!" cried Coco, and out of the corner of her eye Ollie saw Coco swept into a hug by a tall woman with thick ash-colored hair.

Then Ollie and her dad collided, and he managed to stop just in time so he didn't run her over. He caught her to him tightly, and Ollie could feel him shake. "Ollie," he whispered. "Ollie, sweetheart, I was so worried. What happened?"

"I love you, Dad," Ollie said. "I love you."

She buried her face in his familiar flannel shoulder. But right before she did, her watch chimed softly. Ollie glanced down.

LOVE, it said.

"Love you too, Mom," Ollie whispered.

A month later . . .

MS. WEBSTER DIDN'T go to jail. She was supposed to. She went to court and everything. But the night before her sentencing, she disappeared. Ollie, when she heard, wondered if Ms. Webster had made a new bargain with the smiling man, and if so, what it was.

After they left the corn, no one seemed to be able to properly remember what had happened during that night and day. No one except Coco, Brian, and Ollie. There were stories about government cover-ups, about experimental drugs, about aliens.

Ollie and Brian and Coco looked at each other and they shrugged. Was it any less weird than the truth?

Sometimes they talked about it, wondered if the smiling man was still out there, making a new corn maze, making new scarecrows. But mostly they got on with things. They had a lot of living to do.

———

Night fell early in December, and Evansburg smelled like snow, its ponds skimmed over with ice. More ice gathered in the shady places along the banks of Lethe Creek.

But inside Ben Withers Middle School, one classroom was full of light and noise. Two girls sat opposite each other, a chessboard between them, and a whole horde of their classmates stood around, laughing and egging them on.

"Come on, Ollie, you really gonna lose to this city girl?"

"Get it, Coco, get it! Are you letting this know-it-all beat you?"

Neither girl even looked up. They had been playing for half an hour, the last match of chess club practice, but it had turned into a battle, with pieces racing up the board, daring raids, hard-fought exchanges, and clever pincer moves. Both girls tried but neither could gain a decisive advantage.

Now it was the endgame. Ollie was down to a queen, a bishop, and four pawns. Coco had three pawns, her queen, and a rook.

Coco's king was retreating across the board as Ollie jostled him with her bishop.

"Queen's game, Coco," said Mr. Easton. "Watch her pawn—oh!"

Coco had moved her rook. "Checkmate," she said, her eyes glinting.

No one had seen it coming. Everyone froze. Even Ollie did, staring wide-eyed at the board, as Coco's haphazard arrangement of pawns resolved themselves into a clever trap.

Then Ollie whooped, turned her king over, got up, and bowed. "Middle school champion," she said to Coco, and the whole room burst into applause.

Coco flushed with pleasure.

"Rematch tomorrow, though," added Ollie, and grabbed a handful of the popcorn that Mr. Easton had brought for the chess club to eat on the way home.

The girls pulled on caps and coats and heavy boots to a chorus of good nights and set out into the bitter December wind, while Mr. Easton, whistling to himself, locked the school behind them.

Brian caught up with them at the gate. He'd been playing pond hockey; he was grinning like a maniac. "You guys missed out," he said.

"On hockey? Yes," said Coco cheerfully. "Because I love games where I can easily be mistaken for the puck."

Brian snorted. "I'll make you a sign to wear. 'I am not the puck.'"

"Yeah, but hockey players can't read," said Coco, and they all grinned at each other.

"They can sometimes read," said Ollie. "You guys want to come to my house? Dad said he was making his famous corn bread-mole-squash pie. With extra cornbread."

"Only if there's apple pie for dessert," said Brian.

"I can make one," said Ollie. "Dad showed me how."

"Well then, let's go!" said Coco. "Being middle school chess champion makes me hungry."

"Just wait for that rematch," said Ollie.

And so, arm in arm, the three of them walked through the Christmas lights home to the Egg, where Ollie's dad was waiting for them.

"Supper's ready," he said, and smiled.

Acknowledgments

FROM THE DAY I had the idea for a book about kids who get in trouble when their bus breaks down, this story has surprised me. One of the joys of writing *Small Spaces* was going on the journey with Brian, Ollie, and Coco with no notion of how it would end.

I want to thank everyone who got on the bus with me.

To my housemates: RJ, Garrett, Camila, and Blue. You guys put up with my messiness in the living room, my weird crankiness at meals, my eternal sweatpants, my endless empty tea mugs. Thanks.

It's weird to thank a house, but RJ, thanks for buying it, because I would never have thought up the Egg without Slimhouse.

To Dad and Beth, for all those early reads.

To Mom, for telling me I could definitely write two

books at once, even though I wasn't sure I could, and then for reading all the million drafts.

To my agent, Paul Lucas, who thought my weird little story about kids on a bus could actually be publishable.

To Stacey Barney, who also thought my weird story about kids on a bus could be publishable, then proceeded to make it way better and then . . . publish it.

To Evan. For making me all the tea, for being endlessly encouraging, for making me go skiing when I threatened to grow roots in my chair. I love you.